FANGS FOR SHARING

BELLA JACOBS

❀ Created with Vellum

To the Tin Man. For reminding me how much fun playing pretend can be.

One innocent shifter in mortal danger, two dark and domineering vampire princes determined to protect her—but not before they claim her as their own...

The only thing worse than dating a mad scientist who cheated like it was his job? Discovering he secretly revenge-altered my DNA.

Now, I'm a lab-made shapeshifter, the kind hunted by a vicious militant group like it's *their* job. And what The Kin Born catch? The Kin Born kill.

Enter two stupidly hot vampires who say they can give me what I need.

All night long...

Okay, so they don't say the second part flat-out, but we all know what they mean when they say they've been looking for a girl like me. A girl who can handle two bossy alpha vamps in her life. In her business.

In her bed...

But soon our red-hot chemistry becomes so much more. I'm ready to risk it all for these incredible men, but The Kin Born will stop at nothing to capture their prey, and my princes have just moved to the top of their hit list.

FANGS FOR SHARING is a red hot stand alone urban fantasy romance set in the world of Bella Jacob's Dark Moon Shifters series. Each of these steamy standalone tales end with a happily ever after and can be enjoyed alone or as part of the larger Dark Moon universe. No Cliffhanger.

CHAPTER 1

They say love hurts. That it wounds and scars and sucks and bites and is by far the dirtiest trick ever played on humankind—even if it does ensure the continuation of the species.

And right now? Well, I'm totally on board the Love Blows train.

Still, I have to wonder if any of these love-scorning people ever had their ex-boyfriend turn them into a snorting, snuffling, rampaging, shrub-eating, park-pooping, part-time rhinoceros...

Thumbs flying, I jab at my phone like it's a voodoo doll and each letter is a needle stabbed deep in Eugene's lying, cheating, DNA-scrambling face: *This has gone on long enough, Eugene. You've got to change me back. Tonight! Right now! Five minutes ago, even! Put on some pants, I'm coming over.*

Bubbles fill the screen, signaling that my evil ex has finally decided to respond to my texts after a week of radio silence. I stare at my cell, breathless, as—*I'm already wearing pants*—pops up below my rant.

That. *That*'s the part of my message he decides to respond to.

Jaw clenched, I warn, *I'm serious, Eugene, and we both know you're NOT wearing pants. You have that thing about taking off your pants as soon as you get home from work. Which is weird, by the way! Totally weird. And if you're not wearing pants by the time I get there, I'm taking back my Sex Pistols T-shirt, because clearly you aren't cool enough to wear it, anyway.*

More bubbles and then: *Sorry you feel that way, but you're forgetting something, Piglet—you don't know where I live anymore.*

Cheeks heating at the hated nickname—I'm *messy*, not dirty, there's a difference—I dance my thumbs faster. *Ha, that's where you're wrong! Your secretary told me you moved into the faculty housing complex on campus. And believe you me when I say I intend to knock on every door in that building until I find you, and that I won't be shy about telling your colleagues the shitty, no-good, dirty thing you did to me while I'm at it.*

I cross my fingers, praying the threat will be enough to force Eugene to play nice, but his next text lets the air out of my hope balloon pretty quick—*Go ahead. They'll just think you're crazy and call security to have you hauled away, the same way I will if you're unlucky enough to arrive at my door before someone else gets rid of you. And I'll be sure to record every second of your harassment, Pigs. It'll be great evidence for when I file a restraining order against your crazy little ass.*

Huffing hard and eye-rolling even harder, I hurry across the quiet street, forcing myself to wait to start texting again until I'm back on the sidewalk. The east side of the Ballard neighborhood is pretty abandoned this time of night, but with my luck lately, it's best not to take any chances.

Getting run over while I'm texting him would make Eugene happy, and I never want to make Eugene happy. Ever. Again.

Oh please, I tap as soon as my booted heel clomps down on the curb, *be reasonable. I'm not harassing you! I just want to be normal again. The pageant is in two weeks. How am I supposed to break in my new toes shoes and nail my fouetté turn with feet the size of manhole covers? I need my normal body back!*

A smug looking emoji pops up on the screen followed by *Guess you need to work on those anger issues, after all…*

Willing my blood not to boil, I insist, *I don't have anger issues. Or at least I didn't before my boyfriend cheated on me and lied to me and turned me into a rhinoceros as some sort of sick joke.*

An eye-rolling emoji emerges from the bubbles. *Don't be so melodramatic.*

I crushed my car, I shoot back, steps quickening along the damp sidewalk. *I exploded through the windows and burst the doors off and crushed it beneath the weight of my massive rhino body! And insurance doesn't cover destruction by rhino-explosion. Not that I have the kind of insurance that replaces things, anyway, just the kind that fixes things, and there's nothing left of Old Betty to fix. She's gone. Forever. And just FYI, anger isn't the only trigger. I shift when I'm scared, too. A dog ran up behind me in the park the other day, barking his head off, and boom. Full rhino. Right by the side of the jogging path. I shifted so fast I almost crushed the poor thing while I was ripping through my last pair of running shoes and favorite yoga pants.*

Bummer, Eugene replies, with typical lack of empathy.

How on earth did I manage to date this man for six months without realizing he has the emotional depth of a sea slug? A spiteful, vindictive sea slug?

But doesn't sound like it would have been much of a loss mutt-wise, he continues.

My jaw drops. *It was an innocent animal, Eugene!*

With aggression issues.

Stifling the growl gathering in my chest, I type faster. *I'm going to have aggression issues if you don't fix this. Seriously, I could strangle you right now! Or sit on you! With my giant rhino butt!*

Ah-ah-ah...calm down, Pigs, he says, the smug so thick it oozes from the screen. *Wouldn't want you to burst out of that cute little ice-cream scooper uniform of yours. You're still wearing it, aren't you? The pink-and-white pinstripe thing with the itty-bitty skirt and combat boots...*

I swallow the sour taste rising in my throat as memories of me, Eugene, and my skirt—together in sunnier days—rise inside me. There was a time when I thought the three of us might live happily ever after, but that was before I realized how many other women—and skirts—Eugene was involved with. *You don't get to talk about my skirt anymore,* I tap. *My skirt doesn't like you. She thinks you're a douchebag who should put on some pants.*

Aw, come on, now. Don't be like that. Your skirt and I have chemistry, baby. And I think both you and your skirt should relax. You're starting to sound like that man-hating roommate of yours.

I hesitate at the end of the block, looking both ways on Market Street, ensuring I'm still alone before I turn right toward home. I usually wouldn't text and walk so late at night—I've been living in a sketchy part of town long enough to know better than to let my guard down —but I have my last session with my dance coach tomorrow.

I need to be 100 percent human before I head into Jacque's studio. I've been working with my ballet guru since I was a kid just getting started on the pageant circuit after my mother shuttled me off to fat camp to be starved into competition-ready shape. I love Jacque and can't risk causing catastrophic damage to his dance school right before he puts it up for sale this summer.

Without my sweetheart of a coach, and the granola bars he slipped into my dance bag in my teen years, I would have gone to bed hungry even more often than I did already. My mother was a firm believer that beauty and suffering went hand in hand, and that no misery was too great if it meant her daughter went home with a first-place ribbon draped across her heavily padded push-up bra.

I didn't get boobs until I was almost nineteen, a good year after I'd quit the pageant game, moved out of my mother's house, and started eating enough to give fat a chance to settle onto my body again. From there, my new boobs and I forged ahead with college and career—getting a degree in fashion design while selling funky, handmade aprons in my online craft shop and dating boys who enjoyed my new curves as much as I did.

We would have been happy never to set foot, nor boob, on the beauty queen circuit again.

And then I met Leerie in Advanced Draping 201 and became best friends and, eventually, roommates with a fairy—a real live fairy because they do exist, just like shifters and vampires and all the other supernatural creatures people still insist are imaginary, no matter how much evidence piles up to the contrary—and started believing in the power of my dreams. Leerie never cast a spell on me, but living with a friend who supports you, believes in you, and loves you just the way you are has a magic all its own.

Leerie is the sister I never had, and after two years as her partner in spreading sparkle, I'm no longer a dream doubter. I believe in magic and destiny and the power of my two hands to change the world.

But in order to make the kind of difference I want to make—in order to fund my start-up crafting play clothes and costumes for adults in desperate need of fun in their dreary, grown-up lives—I need money, the kind I'm not going to amass working at an ice-cream parlor and selling aprons.

The Miss U.S. Pageant title comes with a fifty-thousand-dollar prize. Last year, as second runner-up, I came within spitting distance of making my dream a reality. Since then, I've killed myself fine-tuning my dance routine, pageant walk, interview questions, and personal essay.

I've been so busy, so focused, that I, admittedly, started phoning it in with some of my nonessential relationships.

I haven't called my mother in months, I barely made

it to my aunt's house for the tail end of Easter dinner, and I continued to date Eugene long after I knew deep down we were never going to be more than friends who banged on Friday nights—when I wasn't too tired from dance practice and work, and Eugene wasn't stuck late at the lab.

Now I know "working late at the lab" was code for "out with other women," but for a long time I felt guilty that I wasn't as into Eugene as he seemed to be into me.

Leerie, of course, knew he was bad news from the start.

If only I'd listened to her.

If only I'd kicked Eugene to the curb before I let him into my room that last night, before we had break-up sex, before he decided to stick an IV needle in me while I was sleeping and rhino-fy my DNA.

Note to self—always listen to Leerie.

Leerie doesn't hate men, I reply, resisting the urge to add "just assholes like you." I've been a part of the pageant world long enough to know the power of a little sweet talk and a call for World Peace. *And I don't hate you. I'm actually hoping we can be friends after this mess is cleaned up. We had fun together, Eugene, and I know we can again. Just fix this, and we'll put it in the past with no hard feelings.*

My reward for this attempt to let bygones be bygones is a laughing emoji with tears streaming out of its closed eyes.

This time I do growl out loud. *Listen, mister, I'M the wronged party, here. YOU cheated on ME. If anyone should be rolling in the mud, binge-eating shrubs, and running from creepy guys with scary neck tattoos, it's YOU.*

My phone rings a second later. I jump.

I can't remember the last time Eugene and I talked on the phone—have we *ever* talked on the phone?—but that's his number, no doubt about it.

And hopefully a call means I've finally gotten through to him.

Fingers double-crossed this time, I hit the green button.

CHAPTER 2

Stomach fluttering, I lift my cell to my ear. "Hey. Can we fix this now? Please? I don't want to fight anymore."

"What did the tattoos look like?" Eugene asks, actually sounding concerned for my welfare, though his question isn't what I was expecting.

I shrug. "I'm not sure. It was dark, and I was running, but it looked like barbed wire or teeth or something, inked in a circle around their necks. Until they turned into wolves, of course. Then I couldn't see the tattoos under all the fur."

He curses beneath his breath. "You have the worst luck of anyone I've ever met. You know that?"

Before I can say something unwise about it being not luck, but my choice in men that sucks, Eugene presses on.

"You've got to stay away from those guys, Pigs. They're not kidding around. If they catch you, they'll hurt you."

"Yeah, I figured that out when one of them stabbed me in the shoulder last night." My pulse stutters as I cross another quiet street, moving farther away from the well-lit commercial area, closer to my shady neighborhood with the chronically malfunctioning streetlights. "If I hadn't had inch-thick rhino skin at the time, it would have really hurt. What kind of gang carries spears, anyway?"

"The kind where they're so strong they don't have any trouble taking people out with a sharp stick," he says, adding in a softer voice, "They could have killed you, Eliza. Seriously. And they'll be better prepared next time. You need to watch your back."

"Next time?" I squeak, fighting to swallow past the lump forming in my throat. "What do you mean next time? Who are those people, Eugene? And why do they want to hurt me? I'm nobody."

"Not to them. And they're not people; you saw that for yourself. They're shifters, the kind that aren't cooked up in a lab. They call themselves the Kin Born. It's their mission in life to take out every shifter who wasn't made the old-fashioned way, and they have enough crooked politicians and policemen in their corner to get away with it. Now that they know you're out there, you'll be on their hit list. They didn't see you shift, did they?"

I gulp. "I don't know. Maybe? These two street kids were torturing a cat, and I got so mad I shifted not far from the ice-cream shop. The tattoo-spear guys came after me a few minutes later. Chased me all the way down Fifty-Fifth, but I managed to lose them in the park."

"Good for you. But you might not be as lucky next time. You should quit your job, change up your routine, maybe move to another neighborhood. Better yet, another state."

Sweat beads on my lip despite the cool spring night, and I beg in a thin voice, "Or you could just change me back. If I'm not a shifter, they won't want to kill me anymore, right? Please fix this? I can meet you at the lab right now. I'll bring coffee, donuts, whatever you want. Whatever you need to power through an early morning DNA unscrambling session."

"You know what I want, Pigs." Eugene's sappy tone assures me I'm not going to like the rest of what he has to say. "You and me. Together. The way we used to be. The way we belong. We're meant for each other, Sparkle Girl."

Tears prick at my eyes, but not because of any lingering feelings for Eugene. I *would* like to be someone's Sparkle Girl. Would like to have someone who really saw me and cared about me. Maybe even loved me, at least enough not to turn me into a rhinoceros without my permission.

"I can't," I say. "It's not going to work, Eugene. Us. You know that. Even before Courtney and Uma, we were struggling."

"Because you were too focused on the pageant."

"Because you were too focused on work," I counter. "Did you really expect me to sit at home, missing dance classes and training sessions, when you were always at least an hour late to pick me up?"

"I would have left work early if you'd asked me to," he counters. "You should have let me know that showing up on time was important to you, Eliza. You've got to learn to communicate. That's what words are for."

I sigh. "You could be right, but the bottom line is we didn't work, Eugene. We're not long-term compatible. We're just too different."

"Especially now." The nasty note in his voice sets my molars to grinding. "Goodbye and good luck, Pigs. It's a hard world out there for an angry girl who's all alone, without anyone to protect her from the big bad wolves."

"No! Don't hang up. We're not finished yet!" I shout, but he doesn't respond, and I know he won't. Eugene likes to have the last word—it's one of the many things that drove me nuts about him.

Sure enough, a second later the line goes dead.

I curse, letting my arm fall to my side.

If only I'd broken up with him sooner. If I had, maybe I could have slipped away without getting on his revenge list. Though, probably not. Eugene isn't the sweet, fun-and-friendly nerd I thought he was when we met at a Snuggly Super Pug comic-signing and costume party last fall. He's a bona fide mad scientist, a sociopath who is fine with putting my life in danger if that's what it takes to get what he wants.

Murder.

I could be *murdered*.

Maybe soon.

So far, I haven't seen any creepy tattooed people with sticks lurking in the darkness tonight, but that doesn't mean they aren't there, just waiting for me to take the shortcut through the park, where they'll be able to slaughter me on the community lawn and devour my intestines in peace, without law enforcement getting involved.

The cops don't step foot in the park after dark. Most sane people don't set foot in the park during the day, either. It isn't a family-friendly green space anymore. I only run there when I don't have time to make it across town to the ritzier running paths, and I always run fast, without headphones to distract me, and with my trusty can of mace clutched tightly in hand.

The only reason I cut into the woods last night was that I knew the twisting trails were my only shot at ditching the guys with the sticks. And because I was a rhino at the time.

That's one good thing about shifting into a creature that weighs more than a city bus—there's not much left to be afraid of. Except for people with guns.

Or shifters with guns…

They could bring guns next time. And even rhino skin isn't thick enough to deflect bullets.

Heart slamming against my ribs, I duck into a covered alcove in front of the closed tattoo parlor at the end of the block, clutching my phone tighter as the real-life implications of Eugene's warning about the Kin Born sink in.

I hide behind a column of bricks, taking another careful peek up and down the eerily deserted street.

When I first starting working part-time at *I Scream, You Scream*, I thought it was cute that a gourmet ice cream parlor stayed open later than the bars and clubs in the trendy east Ballard neighborhood. But that was back when I had a car parked in the employee lot waiting to carry me safely home.

Before I crushed my vintage VW bug to bits.

Before I started going rhino every time my blood pressure rises too high.

Before I heard the faint scuff of footsteps from the alley to my left...

I hold my breath, ears straining, but the night is quiet. Quiet... Quiet for so long that I've nearly convinced myself I was imaging things when it comes again.

Scuff, scuff, and the faint crunch of gravel beneath a heavy shoe.

And maybe it's just an ordinary creepy person stalking me, not a creepy supernatural shifter person who wants to kill me with a stick or a bullet or a missile launcher or whatever it would take to murder a rhinoceros, but it doesn't make much of a difference to my racing heart. A taste like overripe beets floods into my mouth—earthy and thick—and the hair on my arms stands on end as the centers of my bones begin to tremble, signaling a shift is just a few rapid heartbeats away.

"Calm down, calm down," I chant softly, eyes sliding closed as I will my shoulders to relax away from my ears and my jaw to unclench.

I have to stay human.

I have to hold my shit together.

I can't afford to let my imagination get the—

"Don't be afraid." The silky voice hums through the darkness mere inches from my ear, and I squeal, jump half a foot into the air, and explode into a fear-shift, slipping my skin too fast for the fact that the voice is familiar to make one bit of difference.

CHAPTER 3

*I*t is a truth universally acknowledged that a girl's secret crush always shows up at the worst possible moment. *Always.*

Or maybe it's just me.

But you can bet your life, if I've just put on a face mask that smells like cat vomit or shouted for Leerie to toss up a fresh roll of toilet paper because we're out in the upstairs bathroom and my period is trying to murder my vagina, Reagan O'Rourke—Rourke to his friends—is going to be there.

Likely with my less than secret crush, Leo "Crystalline Blue Eyes of a Siberian Husky, Body of a Greek God, and Brain of a Compassionate Philosopher" Poplov, not far behind.

I can usually manage to hide my butterflies with funny, flirty Rourke, but Leo reduces me to a stammering puddle of lust every time.

"Good work," Leo says, making all four of my rhino knees go weak as I waddle out onto the wide sidewalk.

His dry tone gives nothing away, but as he emerges from the shadows of the alley, his Siberian Husky eyes are flashing like pissed-off sapphires, and his manly jaw is clenched tight.

My lips part on an apology, but all that emerges is a bellowing squawk-honk. I don't know if all rhinos screech like giant, frightened chickens, or if that's a side effect of my scrambled DNA, but the contrast between my massive body and derpy voice makes me feel even more ridiculous.

And stressed.

And when I'm stressed, I eat. Before I realize what I'm doing, I've snagged a mouthful of baby spring leaves from the scraggly tree growing through a crack in the sidewalk and am chowing down like my life depends on it.

Rourke, who thankfully isn't dead or crushed, ambles out onto the sidewalk in front of me, cupping my leathery face in one hand with an apologetic smile. "Sorry to scare you, 'Liza. We were trying to keep a low profile, but I guess your hearing is better than it used to be, eh? Even in your human form?"

I nod, chewing faster. I *want* to stop chewing—Rourke is probably grossed out enough by my gray skin and beady eyes without getting a close-up view of my rhino cud—but I can't. I come into this body ravenous. Unless I'm trying to extricate myself from the wind-shield stuck around my neck or running from bad guys, all I can do is eat.

About those bad guys...

I cast a nervous glance up and down the street, another honk-groan escaping without permission.

Weirdly, Leo seems to understand what I'm worried about.

"She's right. We have to find cover. She isn't safe out in the open." He walks to the edge of the sidewalk, eyes narrowing at the entrance to the park on the other side of the street. "Those trees should do for now, but if we see another Kin Born patrol, we have to be prepared to move fast. Even if they can't see us, they'll be able to catch our scent. And we'll absolutely be outnumbered."

"Or she could shift back, and we could just take her home," Rourke says, catching my eye as I grab another bite of skinny elm. Or oak. Or whatever it is. My human self doesn't know much about tree species, and my rhino self isn't picky about what she puts in her mouth.

"Leerie said she can't control it," Leo says. "That's why we're here."

"No, we're here because we care about Eliza," Rourke counters, "and want to make sure she stays in one piece until we can find that twat of an ex-boyfriend of hers and turn him inside out through his left nostril." Rourke winks at me. "We're going to use the left one because I've heard that one hurts more."

I squawk-bleat, and a chunk of half-chewed cud falls from my mouth with a juicy splat, ensuring I'm so mortified I will never laugh in rhino form again.

Rourke pats my neck, seeming not to notice my foulness. But this is the man who taught me how to be a card shark nearly as dangerous as he is himself. He's got a poker face that won't quit and is far too kind to bring attention to embarrassing behavior. But that doesn't mean he's ever going to forget that I almost buried his designer shoe in rhino spit.

"Eugene's not going to get away with this," Rourke continues. "Leo and I are going to make damn sure of it. So you can relax, Princess Pea. Just take a deep breath and let it out slow and easy."

I snuffle and press closer to his hand.

Unlike "Piglet," Rourke's pet name for me makes me feel adorable. He started calling me Princess Pea after last year's New Year's Eve dinner. I was the only one who felt the tiny gift box he'd hidden beneath the cushions of our chairs as a surprise to be pulled out after the clock struck twelve. I'd ruined it by discovering my gift halfway through the salad course, but Rourke hadn't cared. He'd only laughed and insisted I open my present first.

It was an antique bracelet with ballerina-themed charms dangling from a silver chain. I'd worn it all the time, but not since I turned rhino. I don't want to risk breaking such a sweet gift, one of the only presents I've ever gotten from a man.

And yes, the man is supposed to be wooing my roommate, and he has no idea that his dimple and dreamy green eyes do things to me that are far from "just friendly," but I don't care. The gift is still special, almost as special as the present Leo slipped under my door before he left my birthday party last fall. It was a check for fifty-thousand dollars, along with a note saying he wanted to help make my dreams come true.

And even though I will never cash the check—it was too generous of him, and I'm determined to make it on my own—it meant so much that he believed in me.

I glance his way now, wondering if he still believes in me, but his arctic eyes are unreadable. The only hint that he might be anxious is the slight tick at the corner of his jaw and the chill in his fingers as he rests a hand on the other side of my neck.

Contrary to popular lore, vampires aren't usually cold to the touch. Leo and Rourke both run hotter than most humans, a consequence of their faster metabolisms or magic or something that I missed due to the fact that Leo was touching me when he explained it. It was just my elbow, to make sure I didn't take a spill down my front steps in my three-inch heels the last time Leerie, Rourke, Leo, and I went to the opening of one of the bars Leerie did interior design work for, but it was enough to befuddle my brain.

Even now, in a body that doesn't feel like mine, with skin so thick a spear jammed into my shoulder felt about as nasty as a paper cut, the feel of Leo's hands on me—both their hands on me, something that has never happened before, but that I've thought about far too often—makes me dizzy.

Disoriented.

Aware...

So aware that when Rourke leans in to whisper, "Just close your eyes, relax, and know it's all going to be all right," electricity zips across my skin, and my heart beats faster.

But for some reason, even though I'm definitely more worked up than Zenned out, my bones begin to buzz. I close my eyes, homing in on the sensation, one of the early signs that I might be able to go human again.

"That's right." Leo places his other hand on my neck

beside the first. "Exhale to a count of five, four, three, two, one. Now inhale for four, three, two…"

He continues to count me up and down, in and out, and I breathe, following his lead. Amazingly, after only a minute, maybe two, the earthy flavor of an impending shift fills my mouth and—*poof!*—I turn back into a butterfly.

Or into a girl, rather.

A fuzzy haired, sweaty-palmed, naked girl, who instantly slaps an arm over her breasts and a hand down to cover her could-use-a-wax lady parts and turns fire-cracker red.

All the times I've secretly dreamed of ending up naked with Leo or Rourke, it's *never* been like this.

Rourke reaches for the zipper on his jacket. "Hey, there you are. Good job, love, and no worries. We've all been there. Had to walk home buck naked a few years ago after some kids stole my clothes while I was skinny dipping."

"Take this," Leo says. "It should be long enough to cover you."

I look up to see Leo's jacket already on the ground and his white button-up shirt off and held out to me.

He averts his eyes as I slip my arms into the sleeves and whisper, "Thank you," in a post-shift rough voice that's still squawky around the edges.

"Of course." Leo squeezes my upper arm through the fabric. The cotton is still warm from his body, and the touch is so comforting I have to fight the urge to lean into him, rest my cheek on his chest, and sigh in relief.

But considering he's not wearing a shirt—and looks

so beautiful half naked that my pulse is stutter-dancing in my veins—that wouldn't be a good idea. Tingly feelings don't seem to have the same effect on me as fear or rage, but I can't afford to risk another shift. Not only is shifting exhausting and dangerous, but Leo might be less inclined toward sympathy if I ripped through his swanky duds.

Vampires wear ridiculously expensive clothes, and from the feel of this whisper-soft cotton, this shirt is no exception.

I look up at him, still embarrassed, but feeling better now that I'm not the only one who's showing a little skin. "So what now?"

"Now, we get you home," Leo says, "assure Leerie that we kept you safe, and discuss how best to keep you that way."

A long, low howl cuts through the night, echoing through the lonely streets. I shiver. It's hard to tell where it's coming from, but it sounds close. Too close.

Apparently, Leo agrees.

"I'll carry her. You watch our backs," he says, scooping me into his arms before I can protest that I'm fine to run in bare feet. And then I'm so busy marveling at how soft Leo's skin is above all his hard muscle, and how incredibly fast both he and Rourke are able to run, that I can't speak a word.

I simply cling to Leo's neck and watch the cool part of Ballard get farther and farther away, instinctively knowing I won't be seeing it again anytime soon.

CHAPTER 4

*B*ack home, at our cottage set away from the road and hidden by tangles of vines my roommate's green thumb keeps lush year-round, Leerie is waiting by the door.

As Leo climbs the steps, still with me gathered to his chest, I see she's got my robe in one hand and a cup of tea in the other. Her long red curls are backlit by the lamp in the kitchen, and her pale green eyes are blazing with fury. She looks like an avenging banshee, ready to reap the soul of any villain foolish enough to cross her path.

But of course, she's a fairy, not a banshee, and the scariest thing she reaps is massive amounts of mugwort from the garden for her magical herbal teas.

"Tell me you're okay." She shakes her head, sending her curls bouncing. "Or I'm going to hunt down every Kin Born asshole in the greater Seattle metro area and cut their paws off. They didn't hurt you again, did they?"

"No, I'm okay," I say as Leo sets me down in front of the door. "A little shaken, but fine."

"Oh, pumpkin, come here." Leerie motions me into the house with her robe-holding hand, setting it to fluttering in the cool breeze. "I swear I'm going to curse Eugene for this. Give him a fantastic case of genital warts. And scurvy. With a nasty head cold for good measure."

"Thank you," I mumble, shrugging into my kimono-style wrap before casting a glance over my shoulder. "And thanks for sending the cavalry."

Leerie smiles. "Well, even unwanted suitors are good for something every now and then." She circles her arm at Rourke and bare-chested Leo. "Come in, come in. Let me get you two something to drink. I have blackberry-syrup laced O-negative or some straight-up AB positive."

"Positive sounds heavenly, Leerie," Rourke says, his Irish accent lilting into his voice the way it often does around my roomie. Leerie was born and raised in a fairy kingdom in Northern Germany, has lived in the States long enough to have an American accent, and has never set foot on Irish soil, but Rourke swears she's the spitting image of the girl who stole his heart when he was a sixteen-year-old sailor living in County Cork.

In 1756.

Because Rourke is over three hundred years old, a hundred years older than Leerie and a hundred and fifty older than Leo, who wasn't turned until near the end of the nineteenth century.

But you'd never know Leo is the baby of the group.

He's so serious and solemn, while Rourke and Leerie are always ready with a joke.

Especially Rourke.

"What about you, dear 'Liza?" Rourke wraps an arm around my shoulders, giving me a quick squeeze as he moves into the kitchen. "You could probably use something to wet your whistle, aye? Wash the taste of elm out of your mouth?"

My cheeks heat, embarrassment and awareness dumping into my bloodstream as Leo moves around to my other side. They're hard enough to handle one at a time. Having both of them this close is likely to do lasting damage.

My face may never return to its normal color.

"I've got tea for Eliza. Ginger and turmeric with extra honey to help calm her stomach." Leerie sets the tea on our yellow daisy tablecloth and pulls out a chair. "The shifts still making you nauseated?"

"A little." I motion toward the bathroom. "I'll change out of Leo's shirt and be right back."

"I'm sure there's no rush." Leerie casts a disinterested look at Leo's chiseled ten-pack. "He doesn't feel the cold. Do you, Leo?"

Leo shakes his head but doesn't say a word, his jaw still locked tight the way it was the entire dash home through streets echoing with the cries of wolves out for blood. *My* blood. And probably Rourke and Leo's, too. I don't know much about these Kin Born maniacs, but they seem like the kind who would take out their target's friends first and ask questions never.

"There are reasons for wanting clothes, aside from warmth," I say, moving deeper into our cozy home.

"Not all of us are shameless exhibitionists like you and Rourke."

"Skinny dipping is a time-honored tradition among my people," Leerie says in a prim voice at odds with her words. "And swimming is more fun when you're naked."

"Almost everything is more fun when you're naked," Rourke seconds with a wink. "Except boxing. You want something to keep the wangle from dangling in a fight."

I roll my eyes, flustered, but not so flustered I miss the relief in Leo's expression. I meet his gaze, warmth spreading through me when he nods a silent "thank you." I want to tell him that he has absolutely nothing to thank me for—I owe him my life and what's left of my dignity for sparing me a naked, post-shift walk of shame all the way home—but decide that's better left to another time.

A time when Leo and I might be alone...

But of course, we're never alone. It's a crazy thought. He comes to see Leerie, and he always comes with Rourke. They've made it clear from the moment they first started courting Leerie almost a year ago that they're a package deal. Some poor woman is going to have to learn to put up with both of them.

Both of them in her life, in her heart.

In her bed...

Face flaming all over again, I flee to the bathroom before anyone reads my mind. Leerie doesn't have telepathic powers, and neither do vampires, but it takes no supernatural ability to read me. I wear my heart on my sleeve and my thoughts on my face.

After I've changed, I take an extra moment at the sink, meeting my hazel eyes in the mirror, willing them to keep my secrets for another thirty minutes, or however long Leerie and my saviors intend to socialize, and then I head back into the kitchen.

I find Leerie sitting quietly in the chair next to my steaming mug, her face pale and a worry wrinkle checkmarking her smooth forehead.

"You scared her," I accuse the men on the other side of the table.

"She asked how close the Kin Born got to you tonight, and we don't make a habit of lying," Leo says. "If we'd left even a minute later, there's a chance we wouldn't have made it back here alive."

"But you didn't have to tell her that." I toss Leo's shirt at him, refusing to acknowledge the way my pulse leaps as he catches it with a flash of his powerful arm.

"She needs to know," Rourke says in a gentle voice that does nothing to soften his next words. "She could be in danger, too. If those bastards know where you work and the route you take home, sooner or later they're going to figure out where you live. Neither of you is safe here."

"No, I'll make it safe." I slide into the seat beside Leerie, patting her knee under the table. "I promise. I'll quit my job, find another one on the other side of town, and be sure never to take the same way home twice. And, hopefully, shifter-hate won't be an issue for much longer. Eugene is going to change me back soon. He has to."

Leerie turns to me, her pale green eyes cloudy with a chance of rain. "But what if he doesn't, Eliza? I haven't wanted to cross that bridge, but there's a chance he'll refuse to do the right thing."

"Or that he won't be able to do the right thing," Leo adds, bringing the mood in our usually bright and cheery kitchen down another notch. "Some genetic modifications are too extensive to reverse completely. I don't know where a rhinoceros lands on the spectrum, but it seems fairly extreme."

I shake my head. "No, he wouldn't do something he couldn't take back," I insist, ignoring the tiny voice inside that says Eugene seemed pretty ready to let the Kin Born do something he couldn't take back to me tonight. I have to believe this will get better. I can't give in to despair or let rhino become my new reality without a fight. "He can fix this, and he will. He just wants to make sure I suffer first."

"Or die," Leerie adds in a whisper, echoing my own dire thoughts. "He had to have known the Kin Born would find you, honey. It's not like he made you a rabbit or a mouse or something that's easy to hide. He made sure you would stand out. Attract attention."

"The wrong kind of attention." Rourke sets his now-empty wine tumbler down with a sharp *thunk*. "I swear, I could kill the bastard. Skin him alive, inch by inch."

"That might be an option we consider down the road, but for now we need to think more realistically," Leerie says, surprisingly unfazed by the mention of bloodshed. She's usually a hardcore pacifist. But that's how much she loves me—enough to want the blood of my enemies to flow in the streets.

It's special.

Stomach-turning and scary, but special.

"I love you." I squeeze her hand. "Seriously. Thank

you for sticking by me through this. I don't know what I'd do without you."

"And you'll never have to learn," she says, pulling me in for a hug.

"We're here for you, too," Rourke says. "For as long as you need us. We're not going to let you girls face this alone."

"We're not girls." Leerie sniffs as we pull apart, brushing her wild hair back behind her shoulders. "We're capable and clever women. But seeing as neither of us has much experience with violent predators, your assistance would be appreciated."

I nod. "It would. I hate to be a bother, but—"

"Don't be ridiculous," Leo says. "You were betrayed by someone who claimed to love you, and you're in mortal danger as a result. The last thing you should be worried about is whether or not you're a bother."

"He didn't, though," I find myself confessing.

"Didn't what?" Leo asks, confusion in his eyes.

"Love me. He didn't love me." Shame sends my heart sinking like an anchor tossed overboard, even though I know it's ridiculous.

I didn't love Eugene, either.

But still... I would never have put his life in danger.

What's wrong with me that I fail to inspire basic human decency in the men I date, let alone lasting affection?

"It doesn't matter," Leo says after a beat. "You gave him your trust. He should have honored it. And you should have higher standards in men going forward."

I blink, but before I can decide whether I want to

defend myself or admit he's right and that my standards have been perilously low, Rourke cuts in.

"What he's trying to say is that you're the wounded party here, sunshine. And you shouldn't have to apologize for needing help. Especially help we're happy to give." Rourke nudges Leo in the ribs. "Isn't that right, Crankypants?"

Leo arches a brow at the moniker, but the tightness fades from his expression. "That's correct. And we should start by arranging alternative housing for the both of you. My shiver owns rental property throughout the city and surrounding countryside. I'm sure we can get you set up with something suitable."

"Shiver?" I ask.

"A shiver is a group of vampires," Leerie whispers. "Like a flock of birds. Or a crash of rhinos."

"No rhino jokes," I mutter before shifting my attention back to Leo and Rourke, beginning to realize how little I know about their lives when they aren't kicking it human style with Leerie and me. I have no idea where they live or what they do for work or what other social obligations might be part of their lives.

A shiver doesn't sound like a very warm place to belong, but words can be deceiving. Family, for example, sounds lovely until you zoom in and take a closer look at the dysfunction. Both Leerie and I know that from experience. I'm barely talking to my mother, and she and hers have been giving each other the deep freeze for half a century.

"Maybe a building near downtown," Leo continues, "with a doorman and twenty-four-hour security."

"Thank you," I say. "That sounds smart. At least for a little while. If it isn't too much trouble."

"It's just the right amount of trouble." Rourke winks. "Especially if we can get you two in a building with a rooftop pool. It's almost skinny-dipping season, you know."

"I'm not getting in the water until at least June, and surely we'll be home by then." Leerie sighs. "Guess I'll go pack." She pushes her chair back but pauses to point a warning finger at the opposite side of the table. "But no funny business, all right? You find a safe place for Eliza and me to stay—together—and I'll happily pay whatever we owe in rent. This is *not* your chance to get me alone and attempt to pester me into marrying you."

"There's a thin line between pestering and seduction, darling girl," Rourke says, but his heart doesn't seem in it, and when I look his way, I find his attention on me, not Leerie. He looks away so quickly I can't be sure I wasn't imagining things, but the damage is done.

My thoughts are already racing, and my foolish heart is wondering things it shouldn't be wondering about my roommate's would-be boyfriend.

"We'll find a location that will accommodate both of you," Leo assures Leerie. "And Rourke and I will be on our best behavior."

"Best behavior," Rourke echoes, holding up two fingers. "Scout's honor."

"You were never anything close to a Boy Scout, Reagan O'Rourke," Leerie says with a good-natured roll of her eyes. "But you've been a dear friend, and I'm grateful for your help. Though, if you make me regret trusting you with Eliza's safety, *you're* going to regret the day you decided courting me was a good waste of your time."

"Your safety will be our top priority." Leo rises from his chair with his usual grace. "But we should go. Gloria turns in early, and the night isn't getting any younger. There's no need to pack. We can provide anything you need during your stay. Our staff specializes in making shiver guests comfortable." He cocks his head, studying my face in silence for a moment. "And I've got something that might make you more comfortable, Eliza. Help you manage your shifts, give you some control until this is all sorted out."

"That would be wonderful." I stand beside Leerie, the still-warm teacup clutched tight. "Clearly, I need all the help I can get, being a hopeless shifter failure and all."

"You're not a failure," Leo says. "You're new to it. There's a difference."

"And you're not hopeless." Rourke leans back in his chair with a grin. "You're a right lovely little rhino. At least as far as I can tell. Having an aversion to animals in captivity, I haven't seen many rhinos up close, but I'd swing your way at a petting zoo."

"Rhinoceroses aren't petting zoo material," Leerie says, crossing to claim her jacket from the hook by the door. "Neither is Eliza. And just FYI, hitting on my roommate is another excellent way to make sure I never get anywhere close to an altar with either of you."

"You're never going to get close to an altar with either of us, anyway." Rourke glides out of his chair, claiming my hand and pressing a kiss to the back with one graceful movement. "But I apologize, dear 'Liza," he murmurs, his lips moving against my skin, sending inappropriate tingling sensations tickling up my arm. "Can you ever forgive me?"

"Of course," I say with a breathy laugh. "I know you were just joking."

Rourke winks. "Of course, I was." And then he kisses my hand again, leaving me even more flustered than I was before.

Thankfully, Leerie is too busy turning off the lights and grabbing our purses and keys to notice the kiss, but when I glance to where Leo waits by the door, he's shooting Rourke a none-too-subtle glare.

Leo isn't a fan of Rourke's forbidden flirting either, apparently.

I wish I wasn't. Or that I could blame this crush on Leerie's suitors on my scrambled DNA.

But I've had a thing for Leo and Rourke since the moment I met them, the day they showed up on our porch nearly a year ago, bearing gifts and flowers and a letter formally announcing their intention to court Leerie's favor, as required by fairy law. It would be a political and magically motivated union, not a love match, but it doesn't matter. These men are 100 percent off-limits.

So I'm an awful person, as well as a terrible shifter. But at least one of those problems is under my control.

Vowing not to think another impure thought about Leo or Rourke—no matter how handsome and sexy and charming and irresistible they are—I follow Leerie out the door and down the porch steps, leaving our sweet cottage to fend for itself as we head for the vampire-ordered limo idling at the end of the drive.

CHAPTER 5

*T*he Decadence Lounge isn't anything like the vampire clubs I've heard rumors about— dark, creepy, drug-den type places that keep people chained up like anemic cattle to assuage the unholy thirst of the establishments' fanged patrons.

It's more like a 1920s speakeasy, tucked away in a nondescript brick building on the West Side with nothing but a pair of imposing bouncers to hint that it's anything but another abandoned dockside eatery. The speakeasy vibe is solidified as Leo leads us to the back of the warmly lit—and bustling—bar to a vintage cigarette machine. He pulls two handles at once, and a knob appears in the bricks to the right, followed by the outline of a large door.

"Cool," I murmur, unable to keep a grin from my face.

Leo smiles. "Thank you. It's my design."

"Very cool," I repeat, earning a jab in the ribs from Leerie. "What?" I lift my hands in open-armed, nothing-to-see-here innocence. "It is. Who doesn't love a secret passage?"

"Don't encourage him. His head is big enough already," Leerie says, before adding in a faux whisper, "Leo is also the one who invented the internet. He just can't take credit for it, since he was supposed to have been dead and all."

"Impressive." I nod, brows climbing.

"Not as impressive as the fact that Gloria's agreed to see us on such short notice." Rourke opens the secret door, releasing a puff of sweetly-smoky air from the other side. "So let's get moving, lovelies. Don't want to keep the Shiver Master waiting."

"Is that like the queen?" I ask Leerie as we follow Leo through the door and up a flight of stairs.

"Yes," she whispers back. "Each shiver has a line of succession based on bloodline, but a vampire can only stay in power if the group continues to support them in a reasonably democratic way."

"Reasonably?" I arch a brow.

"Sometimes we cast ballots to keep a master on for another quarter century, sometimes the master and a challenger fight to the death," Rourke pipes up from behind us, his voice pleasant considering the subject matter. "But our shivers haven't had a bloody battle for power in centuries. Seeing as we're currently unable to create new vampires, we've become protective of the ones still living. We can't let our numbers get too low, or we risk being absorbed by a larger shiver out to get their fangs on what's ours."

Questions race through my head—Why can't they make any new vampires? How many shivers are there in

Seattle? Why hasn't Leerie filled me in on all this delicious backstory before now?—but it's too late to ask them.

We're here. In the queen's lair.

Or, rather, her office.

It's a really nice office, with a long mahogany board table and twelve chairs to the left, a lounging area with sofas and a flat-screen at the far side of the room, and an adorable art deco bar with crystal decanters filled with the red stuff to my right. But it's still an office, as evidenced by the massive desk that dominates the center of the room.

To say it isn't the romantic, gothic, black-silk-and-red-satin den of sin I was expecting is an understatement.

Gloria isn't at all what I pictured, either.

She's a tiny woman with curly blondish-gray hair and inch-thick glasses that make her already large brown eyes appear owlish as she glances up from the laptop on her desk. She blinks once, twice—as if she has no idea why she's been interrupted—before her lips curve in a big smile and she shouts in a heavy New York accent, "Leo! My baby. My boy, what treasures have you brought me? Such beautiful ladies." She rises from her chair, bustling around the desk with her thin arms outstretched. "Princess Aleerie Nessa the third. Such a pleasure to have you as our guest. Your mother is a dear friend. Can't wait to see her next Solstice."

"Say hello to her for me," Leerie says, leaning down to accept a peck on each cheek. "We're not currently on speaking terms, but I hear she's well."

Gloria's brow furrows, sending her glasses bobbing higher on her nose. "Family trouble, eh?"

Leerie smiles. "Mothers and daughters. Never as easy as one would think."

"Ain't that the truth. Ain't that the truth." Gloria pats Leerie on the shoulder, sending a puff of lavender and rose perfume wafting pleasantly through the air. "Well, at least you've got time to sort it out. One of the benefits of being immortal—you can hold a grudge for a couple hundred years and still have plenty of time to live happily ever after." She cackles at her own joke before abruptly sobering as she turns to me. "No offense to the mortal, sweetheart. I admire you guys. You have to figure yourselves out so much faster. I salute you for it, I really do."

"Thanks so much." I like her more with every passing minute. She reminds me of my aunt Connie, the only member of my family who refused to get sucked into the family or pageant drama.

"This is Eliza," Leo says, coming to stand at Gloria's left, "Leerie's roommate and the one in need of our protection."

Gloria nods, smile widening again. "Yes. Our rhino shifter. Fascinating."

"Less fascinating if you happen to be one," I assure her with a laugh. "But I promise to do my very best not to shift in your office. Or in the apartment where we'll be staying. I don't want to cause any damage."

"The apartment?" Gloria flaps two "get out of here" hands my way. "No, doll face. No way are we letting you shack up in one of our dreary rentals. We're putting you up in the castle. It's all arranged. Sven is getting your rooms prepared, and Jamal will coordinate security and fetch you anything you might need during the daylight hours, when our night staff is underground. You're going to be our guests of honor!"

I start to protest that she really shouldn't have gone to all the trouble—I'm just thrilled to be safe, even if it's in a tugboat apartment docked on the wrong side of the bay—but Leerie subtly kicks my shoe with hers.

"That's very gracious of you, Master." Leerie dips her head. "Thank you."

I drop into a similar curtsy-type pose. "Yes, thank you. So much. It's super awesome of you."

"Super awesome," Gloria echoes with a laugh. "I like that. And I like you, kid." She brings two fingers beneath my chin, lifting my face to hers. "We're going to be great friends. I can feel it."

"I'd love that," I say, meaning it with my entire heart. I don't have many friends—especially sassy, protective older lady friends.

By the time we leave Gloria's office half an hour later, after joining her for a celebratory drink—sour cherry cordial for Leerie and me; the other red stuff for Gloria and the boys—I'm feeling warm and cozy all over, hopeful for the first time since this mess started that everything might be okay.

I don't register the tension in Leerie's expression or the odd silence of the men until we're in the back of the stretch limo, headed toward the hills of the posh part of Seattle in the four a.m. stillness.

"What is it?" I glance between the three of them, wondering what I missed. "I mean...she was nice, right? Everything is fine?"

"Absolutely fine." Leerie crosses her arms, her eyes narrowing. "If you're up for marrying into one of the most violent shivers in the modern world."

"What?" I bleat with a laugh. "What are you talking about?"

"Shall you tell her?" Leerie cocks her head at Leo and Rourke, who are seated on the leather seats facing ours, carefully avoiding eye contact with both Leerie and each other. "Or shall I?"

"It's not true," Leo says softly. "We're not violent. Not often. Anymore."

"But still, kind of true," Rourke counters. "Gloria does like taking care of problems the old-fashioned, murdery way. Makes my shiver look like teddy bears in comparison. Teddy bears stuffed with razor blades, but still relatively harmless, as long as you don't hug us too tight."

"What are you talking about?" My forehead wrinkles. "I mean, I'm used to being the dumb blonde in the room, but I—"

"You're not dumb," Leo says. "You're uneducated in the ways of our world. There's a difference. Stop selling yourself short."

"Okay," I say, holding his gaze, again not sure whether to be touched or irritated by his defense of me. "But I'm in the dark, either way."

"No. You're in the light. You carry it with you," Leo says, in such a matter-of-fact tone that it takes me a beat to realize he's giving me a compliment. A really sweet compliment, in fact. One that has me so flustered that for a moment I can't remember what we were talking about.

Luckily Leerie is immune to vampire sex vibes.

And gorgeous men. And compliments.

"But these two live under a big black raincloud." Leerie reaches for one of the crystal tumblers nestled in a holder on the left side of the limo and fills it with water from an equally fancy decanter. "They're cursed. Have been for...what? Going on a hundred years?"

"One hundred in November," Leo says, studying my face with an intensity that's unnerving.

"What kind of curse?" I shift my gaze to Rourke, who is also watching me closely, though he does a better job of hiding it—pretending to be fascinated by a loose thread at the seam of his jeans while casting glances my way from the corners of his dragon-scale eyes.

"Barren shall thy shivers be, until two princes are united in trinity. Founded in trust and bonded by blood, sealed with the kiss of an Incomparable's love," Leerie says. "Which in layman's terms means they have to find a one-in-a-million girl to take loyalty vows with them, sealing the three of them in vampire marriage for all eternity. If they don't, they'll never be able to make new vampires. Beatrice, the witch who whipped up the curse, wanted them to either learn to play nice or be taken off the field completely."

Leerie takes a delicate sip of her drink. "Beatrice's daughter, the last of the realm-crossing witches, was killed in a turf war between the then-leaders of the Strife and Famine shivers. The kings were both in love with her, and she cared for them, but they refused to share her or territory or anything else. She was caught in the crossfire in a particularly bloody battle and died. Afterward, her mother decided to teach the shivers a lesson. If they don't form a triad with a woman as special as her daughter, they will never be fertile again, and will eventually be taken over by a larger shiver filled with ambitious baby vamps with sharper, pointier teeth."

"Bollocks. My teeth are still the sharpest and the pointiest," Rourke says, before adding in a more serious tone. "And a takeover is still a long way off. The Strife and Famine shivers have ruled Seattle for centuries. Our masters do an excellent job of defending our territory."

"But she's right," Leo says. "Sooner or later, we'll be challenged. And if we haven't broken the curse by then…"

He lets the words hang in the air, and my imagination races to fill in the blanks. "There'll be a turf war," I murmur. "One you could lose if you're outnumbered." Leo inclines his head, and I turn to Leerie. "So this is why they've been trying to get you to marry them? Because you're one in a million?"

"Not one in a million," Rourke corrects. "Absolutely unique. Incomparable. Leerie is the last living earth fairy princess, the only one who can step in to rule Fairy when her mother takes to the ether."

"My mother is never taking to the ether," Leerie says, with a roll of her eyes. "And yes, I am the last living earth fairy princess. But I'm also betrothed."

"To a creep you haven't met," I remind her. "Who is never going to hear you say 'I do,' because he's the worst of the worst."

Tales of her betrothed—a flame fairy with a reputation for brutality on the battlefield and a habit of permanently disfiguring his lovers for his own amusement—are enough to make any sad single girl grateful to be alone.

Leerie takes another sip of her water. "True. But that doesn't mean I'm free to choose another husband. Or husbands. My mother and the other royals tolerate my spinsterhood—for now—but if I were to bind myself to anyone other than my hideous betrothed, heads would roll." She lifts her glass to Leo and Rourke in turn. "Specifically your head. And yours."

"We aren't afraid of fairy vengeance," Leo says, though I can tell his heart isn't in it, "which I believe we've mentioned several times."

Leerie's lips quirk. "Yes, you have. But I don't like to go around inciting a riot for no reason. Seeing as I don't love either of you, and you don't love me, a marriage between us would be far too passionless and boring to be worth spilling blood over."

"Not true." Rourke nudges Leerie's shoe with his boot. "I love you, Leers. You've always been a good friend."

"I don't think friendly love is what's needed to break the curse." Leerie pats Rourke's knee. "But thank you. You're dear to me, too. But if you try to drag Eliza into this mess of yours, I will be forced to cut off your fangs with a meat cleaver."

Rourke winces. "You realize that's nearly as bad as threatening to cut off my balls, right? I mean, a man can survive on bagged blood, but who in his right mind would want to?"

"Indeed." Leerie leans in, giving the water at the

bottom of her glass an ominous swirl. "So think about that before you make any rash decisions."

"Gloria may not be my master, but the Strife shiver is alpha in Seattle, and her word is law," Rourke says, holding Leerie's gaze without blinking. "She decided you were our best bet, so we courted you. But if she's decided there's a better candidate…"

"I'm not joking, Rourke." Leerie's tone is soft but razor sharp. "Leave Eliza alone. She's been through enough."

"Eliza is also right here," I remind her, poking a finger into her side, which fails to break either the tension or the stare off between her and Rourke. I turn to Leo with a sigh. "And Eliza is also still confused. There's nothing incomparable about me. Not by any stretch of the imagination."

"You're the world's only rhinoceros shifter," Leo says.

"Right. Well, there is that." I laugh, but Leo doesn't crack a smile and Rourke keeps right on watching Leerie, like they're gunfighters waiting to see who will draw first. "You can't be serious." I blink, but no one rushes in to assure me this is all a ridiculous joke. "But that doesn't mean anything. I'm a science experiment. I wasn't born this way. And I'm only the only rhino shifter because Eugene hasn't gotten around to making any more of us yet."

"But until he does, you're one of a kind, darlin'," Rourke says.

"But n-not for long," I stammer, ignoring the heat creeping up my throat. "He's going to change me back.

As soon as he's finished being a bitter, sulky little baby man. Could be any day now."

"Or it could be weeks, even months," Leerie says. "Either way, I want a promise from both of you that you won't mess with Eliza. Convince Gloria she's a bad candidate. Tell her she's messy and forgetful and always at least thirty minutes late for everything. Certainly not the kind of person who should be trusted with ancient vampire secrets or the ears of the vampire princes of Seattle."

"Hey!" I give her another fruitless poke. "Not cool. I'm not always late. And I remember things. As long as they aren't birthdays or anniversaries or what we need from the grocery store." I wrinkle my nose. "Or people's names. Or how movies end. Or what I had for lunch."

"Or, if you have to, tell her you're starting to get somewhere with me," Leerie says, ignoring me. "I can pretend to be infatuated with you boys for a month or two—however long it takes to convince Eugene to do the right thing by Eliza."

Leo nods. "I'll do what I can to get Eliza off Gloria's radar. This isn't a world for someone like her."

"Fine," I huff. "If everyone's deciding my future for me, I'll just shut up." I lean back in my seat, lips pressed tightly together, prepared to glare daggers out the window for the rest of the trip. But when I look out, I spot a massive, turreted building at the top of the next hill, illuminated by soft blue lanterns and silhouetted against a sky filled with stars.

It's beautiful. Massive. Gorgeous and majestic and so bleeping cool.

And it's going to be my home for at least the next few days.

In spite of my psycho ex-boyfriend and rhino problems and the evil extremists who want to kill me, I can't help but feel a little like Cinderella. Except I won't have to head home at midnight.

I'll get to stay at the castle, with *two* princes.

Princes who are only interested in me because I'm a freak and their boss told them to be interested, but still...

Is it wrong that I'm a little excited?

We pass through a serious-looking metal gate topped by spikes as long as my arm and guarded by scary-looking men and women, and then stopped twice more for routine safety checks before reaching the top of the hill. Finally, the limo pulls into a circular drive with a marble fountain at its center. We're greeted by half a dozen servants dressed in formal, black-and-white uniforms that would be at home in a costume drama, and a tall, blond man in an impeccably cut suit steps forward to open our door with a flourish and a bow.

"Welcome, your majesties," he says as Leo and Rourke emerge from the vehicle, before adding, "and guests," in a slightly cooler tone that makes me think he's not thrilled to have unexpected company.

"Thank you, Sven," Leo says. "Is the west wing ready?"

"Yes, majesty," Sven says, appraising me with a disdain that makes my skin itch from the inside. "The Lavender and Pennyroyal suites are both prepared."

"Thank you so much for having us." I offer Sven my most dazzling, pageant princess smile as I scoot across the seat and step out of the limo behind Leerie. "We promise not to be any trouble. You won't even know we're here."

"Doubtful, madam." Sven's gaze does a quick sweep up and down my frame as his lip curls ever-so-slightly. "The smell alone... What kind of shifter did they say you were again? An elephant?" He spins on his heel, vanishing so quickly I don't have time to pick my jaw up off the floor, let alone think of a comeback.

But what would I say? Maybe I *do* stink like the rhino paddock at the zoo. I can't smell myself, and Leerie is way too nice to tell me that I reek when there's nothing I can do about it.

I glance ahead, scrambling to come up with a one-liner to turn the snub into a joke, but Leerie, Leo, and Rourke are mounting the impressive steps to the even more impressive front door and clearly didn't hear Sven's stink-burn.

"Chin up, Cinderella," I mutter, hurrying to catch up.

Ready or not, it's time to see what surprises a vampire castle has in store.

CHAPTER 6

*S*tories have power.

　　We're born and bred on stories, tales we've strung together in an attempt to make sense of this crazy business we call life. Sometimes our stories are good magic, helping us rise above adversity and overcome seemingly impossible odds.

But sometimes our stories are the fucking pits.

All the way through the great hall and the tour of the first floor—kitchen, dining room, living room, den, and two separate libraries—I'm trapped in my least favorite story, the one I thought I'd put behind me years ago.

But apparently it wasn't dead, just hibernating, resting up in a dark corner of my mind, waiting for a sneering vampire butler to bring it roaring back to life.

In this story, I am an unlovable "too much" child. Too heavy, too sweaty, too loud, too clumsy—all the toos that led to my mother sending me to fat camp the summer before fifth grade and my metamorphosis into a slimmer, quieter, less sweaty version of Eliza that was deserving of my movie-star-beautiful mother's love.

Or at least, *more* deserving.

Deep down, I knew that the obnoxious, unlovable Eliza was still inside there somewhere, no matter how hard I tried to diet and exercise and discipline her out of existence.

Until I was eighteen years old, I believed I was only worthy of love if I worked my ass off for it. If I changed myself for it.

If I betrayed myself for it.

And then, one day, while at the beach for my senior trip, I almost died saving my friend Lance from a riptide. We were dragged under so many times I never expected to see shore again. I'd only eaten two tiny cucumber sandwiches for lunch—all my insane pre-pageant day diet allowed—and I didn't have the energy to swim hard enough to win a fight against the ocean. Only whole people stand a chance against the merciless pull of the tide, and I wasn't whole. I was a shadow, a mirage. A reflection that was as much my mother as it was myself.

I thought we were goners, but somehow, we made it back from our beach date with death. The moment I collapsed onto the sand beside Lance, I knew that was it. I was done with that old, sad, heartbreaking, soul-crushing story. I was weaving a new web, one big and sticky enough to hold all the pieces of the real Eliza.

But as Leo opens the doors to a stunning ballroom decorated with antique rose-gold chandeliers, all I can think about is my rhino stink.

And how ashamed I am of it.

And how unlovable I am because of it.

And how I wish I were anywhere in the world other than trailing behind two of the most beautiful men in the world and my supermodel-lovely roommate.

"Is that all right with you, Eliza?" Leerie pauses at the double doors on the opposite side of the opulent space and looks back at me expectantly.

I blink faster, emerging from the shame-haze. "I'm sorry, what was that? I spaced for a second. It's been a long night."

"If you're ready to turn in, I can show you straight to your room instead," Leo says. "What I wanted to show you can wait."

I shake my head. "No, I'd love to see more of the house," I say, even though all I want to do is run and hide in the bathroom and take half a dozen showers. But it's rude to refuse your host, especially when he's also a friend and has recently saved your stinky rhino skin from certain doom.

"I'll show Leerie to her room," Rourke says, giving my elbow a gentle squeeze. "See you tomorrow, Princess Pea. Keep your chin up. The world will look brighter after some rest."

His kindness is almost enough to interrupt my shame spiral, but not quite. That's the thing about the inadequacy roller coaster—once you board the ride, it's almost impossible to get off, like trying to climb up a slide covered in Vaseline.

"And I'll be right next door if you need me," Leerie says, leaning down to press a kiss to my cheek. I pay extra close attention to her breath—trying to see if she's holding it due to my wretched stench—but her lips are there and gone too fast for me to judge.

And then Rourke and Leerie are gone, too, disappearing down a warm, wood-paneled hallway to the left as Leo gestures to our right. "It's this way. The stairs to the armory are just before you get to the servant's quarters."

The armory? We're going to look at weapons?

This is not what I was expecting, but that's what you get when you stop living in the now and miss chunks of pertinent conversations. I've got to get my head on straight.

I'm safe in this heavily guarded fortress—for now—but I have to return to my normal life sooner or later. And when I do, there are militant shifters out there straining at the leash to kill me.

Not to mention the pageant in two weeks or the rent due in three or the fact that I've only got a month of emergency money saved up and will need to find a new job ASAP. Especially if I don't win the pageant, which isn't a given, even if I manage to stay human through the entire event—which is also not a given.

Beauty queens can be vicious. Keeping your temper after a girl has swapped your hairspray for foam adhesive or smeared your stick-on bra with enough Muscle Freeze to make it feel like your boobs are going to melt off your chest during the evening gown competition, is easier said than done.

Besides, I'm not a sad little girl desperate for her mother's love anymore. I'm a grown woman who loves herself and her friends and still has plenty of love left over to march to end animal testing and volunteer at the Boys and Girls Club in the summer.

Vowing to put the past back where it belongs, I follow Leo around the corner, down a long, curved set of stairs, and into another space that isn't at all what I expected.

CHAPTER 7

I stumble off the last stair, jaw dropping as I take in what looks like the world's largest—and most fabulous—walk-in closet. "Oh wow."

Leo's lips curve on one side. "I thought you'd like it."

"Like is not the word. I *love* it. It's incredible." Walls painted a tasteful gold set off white built-in shelving units that line the large room. Modern suits of armor—padded and shielded body suits—mingle with shimmering evening gowns, period costumes, and a row of blue jeans in various washes. Mirrors surrounded by softly glowing lights are set at an angle in each corner, and back-to-back overstuffed cream couches dominate the center of the room, reminding me of the "boyfriend chair" outside the typical department store dressing room.

And though there *are* guns, axes, and swords on some of the shelves, there are just as many displays of shoes, accessories, and an entire purse section that has my inner bag-collector salivating as we move farther into the space.

"So it's one-part armory, one-part communal closet of awesome?" I ask, fingering a pale pink gown with seed pearls sewn into the chiffon skirt.

"Not exactly," Leo says, his hands sliding into his pockets. "All of the clothing here is weaponized in one way or another, even that seemingly sweet pink dress."

I snatch my hand back with a grimace.

Leo laughs. "Don't worry. The pearls don't become poisonous until they're mixed with liquid and an activating agent stored in hidden pockets right...here." He motions to the neckline of the dress, and I can't resist leaning in and lifting the fabric gently away from the hanger.

"Genius," I murmur, spotting the two discreet pouches sewn into the lining near the built-in bra. "Though I'm glad pageant contestants don't have access to poisonous dresses."

"Agreed. That would be dangerous."

I glance up at him in surprise. "You're familiar with the pageant world?"

"No. But I'm familiar with the lengths women will go to when forced to rely on their appearance to gain power. Brutal doesn't begin to describe it. The things they'll do to themselves... To each other."

"It can be brutal," I agree. "But in most situations, women are still judged primarily by the way we look—at work, on social media, dating apps, when we're walking around existing after forty or fifty or whenever society has decided we're no longer sexy." I shrug. "At least in a beauty pageant I know when the judging's coming and there's a prize at the end if I win."

Leo's arctic gaze settles on my face. "Or you could have accepted my gift and never had to prance across another stage again."

"I don't prance, I glide," I murmur because I'm not sure what else to say. When we talked a few months ago, Leo seemed fine with me refusing his check, but now I'm thinking I might have misjudged his reaction. "And it was too generous, Leo. I couldn't accept that much money from a friend, not without knowing if I'm ever going to be able to pay it back."

"It was a gift, not a loan, Eliza. I didn't care if you paid it back."

"Well, I do," I insist. "And I can't be sure I could. I have zero experience running a clothing manufacturing business. There's an excellent chance it will crash and burn."

"It won't. You're too good at what you do. Your clothes are perfect."

"You've only seen the mock-ups and drawings," I say, my cheeks heating with pleasure at the compliment. "I could fail in the execution, and then *Play Time* will be just another start-up that didn't get off the ground. Maybe grown-ups don't want to play dress up as much as I think they do."

"People are starved for play," Leo says, holding my gaze. "For joy. For the light you could already be shining into the darkness if you'd let me help you instead of being pointlessly stubborn."

"It isn't pointless," I say, standing up straighter. "I want to succeed on my own. To prove I've got what it takes without cut corners or sneaky cheats. And a no-strings loan from a rich friend is definitely a sneaky cheat."

"Gift, not a loan," he repeats, proving he's every bit as stubborn as I am. "And if you look at it that way, you shouldn't enter the pageant, either. It isn't fair, after all, that you were born beautiful and graceful and clever when so many women were not. You've got an unfair advantage."

I tuck my frizzy hair behind an ear, too flustered by the compliment to come up with anything clever to say in response. "It's not the same thing," I mumble before quickly changing the subject. "And I won't be winning any pageants or starting any businesses if I don't stop crushing things with my rhino butt—and get better at choosing boyfriends."

"Yes, better boyfriends. A point on which we can agree." He clears his throat and nods toward the back of the room. "And why we're here. I've got something that should help you regain control of your shifting."

"*Regain* infers that control ever existed," I say, following him to a display case filled with sports equipment.

"Gain control, then." He plucks a weathered, vintage-looking baseball bat from between a pair of sleek pool cues and a golden baton with diamonds set into the padded ends. He holds the bat out to me, balanced on his open palms. "For you."

"Thanks so much," I say, trying not to eye the shiny

baton. I wasn't raised by wolves, for God's sakes. I would never be so rude as to refuse a gift—or ungrateful enough to ask for a different present—but I can't help thinking that a girly blonde walking around with a baton would be a lot less conspicuous than one toting a tired old bat.

But my opinion of the weapon is transformed the moment I lift it from Leo's hands. It's like picking up a two-hundred-dollar ceramic curling iron imported from Japan—instantly clear that I'm holding a finely-crafted tool. It's heavy, but not too heavy, and the slim handle feels like it was made for my hands. The smoothly polished wood warms appealingly beneath my fingers, and as I lift it to my shoulder, I can feel my badassery level increasing.

"Nice." I wiggle my hips back and forth, getting a feel for the bat's balance. "Thank you so much."

"Don't thank me until you learn what it can do," he says, guiding me in front of the mirror with a hand at the small of my back while I willfully ignore the way his touch makes me fizz. "This is no ordinary bat."

"Well, duh," I say, loving the way his eyes crinkle at the edges in response. Leo is a gorgeous man at all times, but when he smiles...be still my sizzling panties.

"Right," he says. "Duh, indeed. Pearl clearly has special powers."

"Her name is Pearl?" I barely stifle a squee. "I love it. And I will be very good to Pearl, I promise."

"And Pearl will be very good to you."

"Because she's poison," I guess, meeting his gaze in the reflection.

He rolls his eyes. "No, she's not poison."

"Easy there, Mr. Eye Roll, I was kidding."

His brows arch. "Were you?"

"I was," I say, enjoying the teasing banter more than I should. But then, a little flirting never hurt anyone. "My real guess is that Pearl possesses super strength." I circle my hands, sending the bat spinning slowly over my head. "She magnifies the force of my swing, enabling me to knock bad guys over the wall and out of the park."

"Closer," Leo says, crossing his arms. "But not quite."

"A hint then?" I'm a creative thinker, but it's late and I confess I have a limited imagination when it comes to ways to use a bat, even a super-powered one.

"Pearl is very sensitive to how you're feeling." Leo reaches into his pocket, pulling out a tennis ball he must have plucked from the case when I wasn't looking. "For example, if I told you this ball was rigged to explode on impact and then threw it at the mirror—" He throws the ball, and my pulse leaps like a horse busting out of the gate at the derby.

My lips part on a warning for Leo to stand back, certain I'll be going rhino, but the words emerge as a soft cry of surprise as Pearl ignites over my shoulder. White flames burst and sizzle around her tip, but I don't sense any heat, only an intensification of the warm, pleasant sensation I felt when I first picked her up.

Best of all—I don't shift.

"Pearl is fueled by emotion," Leo says, shifting to the right, out of the glare of the glowing weapon. "She takes your fear and anger and draws it into herself, leaving you clear-headed and ready to swing with focus and clarity."

I pull in a breath and let it out, my chest rising and falling without tension. "You're right. I feel relaxed. And I'm still me!"

He nods. "You are. Pearl will help keep you human until you're ready to shift. And if you do need to fight back, when you hit your target, they'll feel it. A couple blows and your average Kin Born shifter will be out cold. Pearl doesn't kill, but she turns the lights out pretty damned quick.""

"Thank you so much, Leo," I say again, with more feeling, my heart full of gratitude that makes Pearl flare brighter. "Um, so what do I do with a charged Pearl if there isn't any butt around that needs kicking?"

He smiles. "Just relax your grip."

I loosen my hold on the bat with one hand, then the other, and the flames flicker out, leaving Leo and I in the honey glow of the fancy dungeon lighting once more. I let Pearl slide through my hands until I'm gripping her around the middle then hug her close. "We're going to get along great, Pearl. Even if you aren't a baton."

Leo's smile fades. "The baton isn't for you. Or anyone else."

I spin to face him, heart stuttering. "Of course. I was just kidding, Leo. I'm so grateful for the gift. I didn't mean to—"

"If I had my way, it would be destroyed, along with everything else that belonged to her," he continues, his hands curling into fists at his sides. "But I'm second-in-command. I don't get my way. The Master decides what goes and what stays." His eyes catch mine; all the warmth has vanished from their depths. "You should remember that while you're under this roof. Her spies are everywhere."

I swallow, fingers tightening on Pearl's smooth length. "Why would Gloria be spying on me?"

"She spies on everyone, and you know exactly why you're on her radar," he says, the muscle in his jaw ticking. "If you're not interested in going along with her plans, then I suggest you make damn sure you don't give her a reason to think you'll come around to seeing things her way."

"What does that mean?" I ask. "That I shouldn't talk to you or Rourke?"

"You can talk." He stalks closer, making me feel like a mouse that's wandered into the feral cat room at the animal shelter. "But that's all. You talk. You don't smile. Or bat your eyelashes. Or giggle when Rourke is stupid enough to kiss your hand. Or lean over a little too far when you're wearing a low-cut shirt."

My jaw drops as I sputter, "I never—"

"Of course you have," Leo cuts me off. He's close enough that he looms over me now. "And the view down your shirt is beautiful," he continues in a silkier voice, one that makes my traitorous body ache. "You're a lovely woman, Eliza, in every way. But this life isn't for you. You don't belong in the darkness."

"It doesn't seem so dark to me," I hear myself saying, even though I agree with him.

I don't want to get tangled up with one vampire, let alone two. Vampires, even in this relatively civilized time in their history, are dangerous. And the emotionally manipulative, unavailable people in my life have given me a hearty fear of commitment. I'm cautious with my human relationships, let alone bonds that could last thousands of years—even eternity, if you're good at staying out of the sun and avoiding vamp conflict.

But there's something in Leo's eyes, in his tone when he said the view was lovely... That *I* was lovely.

Something that makes it hard to listen to the voice of reason.

I don't want to turn my back and walk away. I want to lean in, wrap my arms around Leo's neck, and find out if his lips are as soft as they look.

"And that," he whispers, fingertips brushing my cheek as he tucks a rogue curl behind my ear. "Definitely don't do that."

"Do what?" I ask, though I have a pretty good idea. He's talking about sex eyes and the hunger pulsing through my veins, the hunger I'm sure he can see on my face as clearly as I can see it on his.

Leo wants me. The realization is breathtaking.

He wants me even though he doesn't *want* to want me, which is the most seductive wanting of all. What woman doesn't want to feel irresistible to a gorgeous man? A good, gorgeous, intelligent man she's always assumed was so far out of her league he might as well be another species?

But then, in a way, he is—I'm reminded of that when he wraps his hands around my waist and lifts me like I weigh less than Scrawny Sheila, first runner-up at Miss Seattle and the reason God invented sandwiches. She needs a sandwich as badly as I need Leo to pull me close, crush his lips to mine, and show me what it's like to kiss a man who's as clever and kind as he is drop-dead gorgeous.

But Leo doesn't draw me in. He moves me carefully away, putting a good two feet between us before he sets me down. "Sven will show you to your room. He's waiting at the top of the stairs."

"Oh, o-okay." I cast a flustered glance over my shoulder, but the heavy door to the armory is closed and the top of the stairs invisible from here.

"I can hear him," Leo whispers, answering my unspoken question. "Eyes and ears are everywhere, Eliza, and this isn't going to happen. I learned my lesson about beautiful, fragile things the hard way." He takes another step back, his head dipping in a gentlemanly bow that does nothing to soften the blow of rejection. "I'll see you after sunset. Get some rest and think about what it will take to convince your ex to do the right thing. Rourke and I can be persuasive when the occasion calls for it."

His lips part, revealing newly long, sharpened incisors. I've never seen Leo in attack mode before— vampire teeth look like human teeth most of the time— but it doesn't scare me. It should, of course. Any reasonable woman confronted with clear evidence that the man she's with could chomp her neck in half like a giant mosquito would run screaming.

But his potential for violence only makes the buzz inside me hum louder, my nipples pull tighter, and the ache inside me do some shapeshifting of its own.

Until lust becomes something closer to longing...

"Good night, Eliza," Leo says, a warning in his voice.

"Good night." I hug Pearl close as he walks away, moving so quickly he's gone before I can think of anything else to say.

Which is probably for the best.

Nothing I want to say is a good idea, anyway.

CHAPTER 8

*D*espite the thick black-out curtains in the Lavender room—a sumptuous suite complete with Victorian antiques, decadently comfy bedding, a coffee bar, and a state-of-the-art treadmill by windows overlooking Seattle and the bay beyond—sleep is impossible.

I'm exhausted but keyed up at the same time.

I should be fretting about Eugene, and the Kin Born shifters who want me dead, and the fact that the pageant is rapidly approaching and there's no way I'm going to be competition-ready at this rate—not if I don't start hitting the rehearsal room more than I do the donut shop. But those worries aren't what keep me tossing and turning for hours on end.

My thoughts are of the look in Leo's eyes, the emotion in his voice as he implied that I was on his list of beautiful, fragile, desirable but forbidden things.

Finally, around ten in the morning, I drift into a fitful sleep, plagued by dreams of giant spiders and frogs that shoot poison out of their eyeballs—two of my usual anxiety dreams—but when I wake around four in the afternoon, Leo is still taking up an inordinate amount of room in my thoughts.

I've always been too curious for my own good, and everything about the way Leo was acting last night has my inner cat in the mood to paw through the sand until she finds the good stuff.

I take a quick shower and dress in a sinfully soft, pale pink velvet tracksuit I find in my closet, leaving my hair to air dry as I pad across the hall to Leerie's room and knock on the door.

"Come in, Eliza," she calls.

I wrinkle my nose as I pop inside, shutting the door behind me. "How did you know it was me?"

Leerie, decked out in a dark green maxi dress that sets off her fiery hair, is lounging in a padded armchair in front of her open windows, reading what looks like a very old book. She lifts her gaze, smiling at me over the top of the pages. "You knock like an Eliza, of course. How did you sleep?"

"Good," I lie, crossing to the sitting area and crawling into the overstuffed chair next to hers. "But something's bothering me. Something Leo said last night while we were in the armory."

"How did that go?" She tucks a tissue into the book to mark her place and sets it on the table between us. "I assume he gave you a weapon of some kind? Something to help with the shifting? I'm so curious. Vampires have the best weapon collections, the Strife shiver, especially. I believe they even have a few fairy-forged defenses, which are ridiculously rare. My people usually keep all the good stuff for themselves. Did you see any glittering dresses? Something in silver or gold, maybe, with the power to make the person wearing it disappear?"

"Maybe," I say, even though I absolutely know what she's talking about and could point her to exactly where the dresses are. But Leerie and I have been friends a long time, and I know better than to give my tight-lipped roomie information she wants before I've used it for leverage. "Want to play I'll show you yours if you show me mine?"

Her eyes narrow. "That's nonsense. And no, I don't want to play that game. Whatever it is, if Leo wanted you to know, he would have told you himself. And I don't like to gossip."

"Not true. You love to gossip, as long as it's some-thing you want to gossip about." I swing my legs up and over the arm of the chair, pointing my toes in their cushy white tennis shoes. "Like, enchanted fairy dresses I might have seen, for example…"

Leerie grunts. "Fine. One question. That's it."

Resisting the urge to clap my hands, I ask, "Leo said he learned his lesson about lovely, fragile things the hard way. What does that mean?"

"He said that to you?" Leerie's brows shoot up her pale forehead, and heat creeps into her eyes. "After I warned him and Rourke to keep their hands off of you upon penalty of penis chopping?"

I grimace. "I don't think you put that fine a point on it."

"That's what I meant, and they both knew it. And yet Leo still decided it would be a good idea to come on to you while my back was turned."

"He wasn't coming on to me," I huff. "It was the total opposite. He was pushing me away."

Leerie's eyes go wide, but I cut her off before she can threaten to amputate any parts of me, "I wasn't coming on to him, either! We were just talking about how I should behave while I'm here, how to make sure the master realizes that Rourke, Leo, and I are never going to be more than friends."

She *harumphs* as if she isn't quite buying that, but when she speaks her voice is more relaxed than it was a moment before. "That's a good suggestion. Gloria already has enough ideas. No need to encourage them."

"Right," I agree, nodding. "So...the lovely and fragile thing?"

Leerie sighs. "Oh, that... It's not a happy story, I'm afraid. Fifty or sixty years ago, before the shiver prince in line ahead of Leo was killed and Leo advanced to second-in-command, he was married to a mortal woman. Her name was Eleanor. She was a brilliant artist, a sculptor. The sort who could chip away at solid rock until it softened and gave up all its secrets."

I cross my arms, sensing that she's talking about stony Leo as much as literal rock. "So she was good for him."

"Very good, at least from what I hear." Leerie glances out the window, where the sun is beginning its leisurely, late-spring descent toward the horizon. "According to the gossip, they were very much in love and very happy and in the process of adopting a child. Leo using an assumed identity, of course, to explain why a centenarian was looking so spry."

My stomach twists. "But something went horribly

wrong. Just tell me. Quick. Like ripping off a bandage. You know I hate bad suspense."

"The Strife shiver can't make new vampires until the curse is broken," Leerie says, still watching the sun. "So Leo couldn't offer his wife immortality or the enhanced strength and magic of a vampire. But even if he could have given her the Blood Kiss, rumor was Eleanor would have refused it. She wanted the sun, mortality, a human life, even though it meant she would eventually die, while Leo remained on this plane without her."

"So she died of old age?" I ask hopefully, though my gut is assuring me that's not how this story ends.

Leerie turns back to me. "No. She was murdered. By vampire hunters, they think, though they never caught the monsters who slaughtered the woman Leo loved and left pieces of her scattered through their home."

I cover my mouth with my hand.

"They say there was an organ in every room," Leerie continues, "and they found her head on a pike in the middle of their garden, in a patch of night-blooming jasmine."

"Oh God," I whisper. "Poor Leo. Poor Eleanor."

"Loving a vampire is dangerous," Leerie says. "And it isn't just the vampire hunters or other supernatural species you have to worry about. It's other vampires— from rival shivers, even from your own family—who decide to clear a path to the power or status they crave." She pauses before adding in a softer voice, "A vampire prince is an especially appealing target for the ruthlessly ambitious."

Swinging my legs off the arm of the chair, I sit up

straight, hands balled into fists on my thighs. "You think someone might want to hurt Leo?"

"Kill him," Leerie corrects. "And I'm sure more than one someone wants exactly that. Rourke isn't safe, either. The Famine shiver isn't as cutthroat as the Strife, but Rourke's been the prince for nearly eighty years without finding a woman both he and the Strife prince can agree on. His superiors were understanding for a time—everyone knew Leo was grieving the loss of his wife and that a one-of-a-kind woman is hard to find—but patience is wearing thin. The Strife and Famine ranks are dwindling, and neither can replenish their shiver until the curse is broken. If Leo and Rourke don't seal the deal soon…"

"You knew that and you still let them come sniffing around our place," I say, shocked at my usually kind-to-a-fault friend's behavior. "When you knew for a fact you were never going to marry either of them? Let alone both of them?"

"I didn't *let them* do anything," Leerie says calmly. "Leo and Rourke are their own people. If I said 'never' and they chose to assume I meant 'maybe,' that was their choice. We've been friends since long before I was the only living earth fairy princess. They should know better than to think that when I say' no' I mean anything other than just that."

My lips part, but words stick in my throat as I digest the information hidden in that confession. "What do you mean before you were the only living princess? You've never mentioned a sister."

She lifts one bare shoulder and lets it fall. "Tatiana and I were never close. She was younger, from a different mother, a bastard raised to believe I was the only thing standing between her and the status she deserved."

"What happened to her?" I ask, before adding quickly, "You don't have to tell me if you don't want to. If it's painful to talk about."

Leerie's lips curve ever so slightly. "It's not painful. Just sad. Like I said, I didn't know her well. We only saw each other two or three times a year, at court festivals where it would have been an insult to my parents for any of the court's children not to attend. Even the bastards were expected. My mother has two bastard sons, as well. Boys can't inherit the throne, so Soren and Bale and I have always been good friends." She stands, crossing to the coffee bar beside the window. "But Tatiana was born bitter and jealous and the cousins who raised her encouraged it. They hoped to have her ear if she gained the throne and influence her to take our people in a direction less peaceful than my parents have favored for the past thousand years."

My shoes sink into the thick carpet as I lean forward. The suspense is killing me, but this story clearly isn't easy for Leerie to tell, and I don't want to rush her.

"Everyone expected Tatiana to issue an official challenge to the line of succession sooner or later." Leerie fills the coffee maker's reservoir and drops a pod into place. "If she had, we would have fought to the death in front of the court. Whoever was still breathing at the end would have dethroned my mother and been declared queen."

"Jesus." I press a fist to where my heart is beating fast. Not fast enough to force a shift, but enough that I wish I'd brought Pearl with me, just in case. I make a mental note to go grab her as soon as the story is finished and say, "But you didn't have to, right? They didn't make you kill your own sister?"

Leerie snaps the lid down onto the pod with a sharp click. "No, I didn't. My father arranged to have her murdered in her sleep before she could issue the challenge." She turns, her expression eerily calm as she adds, "That's the thing Tatiana never understood. My father loved her, yes, but he loved me more. He's a good man, but he plays favorites. So when my mother told him to take care of the problem…he did."

I stand, hurrying across the room to pull Leerie in for a hug. "Wow, mama, I'm so sorry. That's just… awful. I hate that you had to go through that. That you're *still* going through that." I pull back, peering up into her face. 'That's why you and your mom aren't speaking, I'm guessing?"

She nods. "And why I don't go home for solstice anymore. I think I could have talked Tatiana out of fighting to the death. Either before the challenge or during. At least I would have had the chance to save her. But now her blood is on my hands."

"That's not true." I shake my head. "You're not to blame for any of that. Not one little bit."

"But I am," she says. "I'm a princess, and with great power comes great responsibility."

"Isn't that Spiderman's theme song?"

"It's a motto, not a song," she says with a sniff. "And yes, it is. You know I can't get enough of men in tight red jammies."

Before I can suggest a Spiderman marathon to help

while away the rest of the afternoon—and put our thoughts in a happier place—there's a soft knock at the door and Leerie calls, "Come in, Jamal."

I frown, and she smiles, adding, "He knocks like a Jamal, of course."

I turn to see a curly-haired man with dark-copper skin, a jaunty black goatee, and kind brown eyes waving from the door. "Sorry to interrupt, princess, but I've been sent to fetch your lovely companion. Prince Rourke has a surprise for her in the annex."

I glance up at Leerie, but she shoos me along. "Go. Have fun. I'll see you at dinner. I think the boys have something romantic planned in the garden. But their plan will fail, of course, now that we're both immune to romance."

"Completely immune," I lie.

Leerie arches a brow. "Just keep one foot on the ground, pumpkin. And remember this is all temporary for us. We have simpler, easier, lovelier things waiting in our futures."

I nod, determined to be as grounded as Leerie. Someday. Maybe by the time I'm two hundred.

I hug her goodbye and follow Jamal out of the room into the hall, headed for a surprise I can't help but be excited about. Almost as excited as I am to see Rourke and Leo again once the sun finishes its seductive slip below the hills.

CHAPTER 9

$\mathcal{J}$f Sven is a glass of prune juice with extra lemon, Jamal is a fine pinot noir—one sip and you know you've found something you'll want to enjoy for a while.

He's one of those effortlessly charming and efficient people who seems to light up the world wherever he goes. As we make our way downstairs, he texts the gardeners about a problem with the duck pond, pauses to adjust flower arrangements, and offers compliments to the window washers and household staff, all while making me feel like the center of his attention with frequent smiles and amusing stories.

"And since that fateful day, not a single four-legged friend has set foot in the castle out of respect for Belinda's sacrifice," Jamal says, as we pause near the exit to the great lawn, in front of a portrait of a woman with long golden hair and a lap full of corgis.

I nod slowly. "Wow. So...vampires can survive on animal blood?"

"Survive, but not thrive," Jamal says, "which is the reason only six of the twenty souls trapped in the castle during the Siege of Bethel's Coven survived. Belinda, sadly, was not one of them. Couldn't bring herself to feed on her babies." He clucks his tongue. "I can't say I'd be any different. My little Jezebel is my world. I'd rather chew off my own hand than harm a hair on my darling's sweet head."

"What breed is she?" I ask, following him through the French doors and out into the warm evening.

"Rescue mutt." He flashes his almost impossibly white teeth, and I wonder who does his bleaching. My pearly whites could use an equally super shine-up before the competition. "With a heavy dose of miniature pinscher. She has the most adorable spindly legs. Like a fawn. So elegant and ladylike."

I grin as I motion toward his suit coat pocket. "I know you have pictures."

Jamal laughs. "Oh, I do. But if we start that, I'll never get you where you're going. I'll pull up my favorites tonight, and we can have show-and-tell tomorrow afternoon when I bring your breakfast." He cocks his head, shooting me a discreetly curious look from the corners of his dark eyes. "I'm assuming you'll be on vampire time during your stay? The better to enjoy your hosts' company?"

"Yes, I suppose so." I twine my fingers together in front of me as we cross the wide, luscious lawn, bound for an outbuilding with a roof shaped like a circus tent. "Though, I'm hoping my stay won't be too long. I'm so grateful for the hospitality and protection, but I have a life to live and bills to pay."

"Oh, the bills are taken care of, sweetie." Jamal waves a breezy, heavily-ringed hand. "That was the first item of business on my list this morning. Mr. Poplov may be a prince with unlimited resources, but he remembers what it's like to live a human life. You're in good hands with him." He clears his throat before adding in a voice almost too soft to hear, "Not like some of the others."

"Like who?" I ask. "Leerie was telling me this morning how dangerous vampire politics can be. Is there anyone I should be careful of? Avoid if possible?"

"Oh everyone, darling," Jamal murmurs, shielding his mouth with his fingers as he adds, "especially the people in charge. Don't buy their folksy routine for a hot minute. They're the worst of the worst. Agendas for days."

"Oh yeah?" I ask, chewing on the corner of my lip. "Not even the master?"

"She's definitely got her own priorities," he says, the merry light fading from his eyes. "But if you keep your guard up and aren't afraid to defend yourself, you'll be fine. Survivors always survive, even during times of upheaval. At least, that's what I've seen in the two hundred years I've been serving the castle."

My jaw drops, but before I can ask how he's lived that long without being a vampire—that we've made it all the way across the sunny grass to the circus-tent building without him catching fire proves he's not—he winks and wags a finger. "We'll have time for gossip later. Now get in there and show this man what you're made of." He taps my chin lightly until my lips close.

"There you go. Pretty as any picture and three times as lively. You're going to slay those other pageant girls."

I blink. "How did you know? About the pageant?"

"I know a lot of things." He sweeps aside his thick brown curls to reveal a third eye in the center of his forehead, this one bright blue instead of warm brown. "And from what I'm seeing so far, you've got an excellent chance at claiming that crown, girl."

I nod, playing it cool, pretending I'm accustomed to new friends revealing their extra body parts on first acquaintance. "Oh. Well. Good. That's great. Thanks so much."

Jamal's third eye winks at me with a sassiness in keeping with the rest of him. "Good luck." He tugs his buzzing phone from his pocket. "Now, I've got to jet. Looks like those ducks have decided they don't want to be relocated to the south side of the pond, after all."

"Thank you." I wave as he backs away, waiting until he turns to walk briskly across the lawn toward the water glittering in the near distance before pulling my own phone and jabbing out a text to the man standing in the way of pageant gold.

I almost died last night, Eugene, and I know that's not what you want. You're a good person, not a murderer. Please, let me meet you tonight, at the university lab or wherever you'll be able to fix me without getting in trouble. I don't want you to lose your job or your license, I just want my life back. We can move past this and be friends and no one ever has to know. Okay?

I stare at the screen, willing him to reply. But there are no words, no bubbles, no sign of a response. My ex is clearly back to being an uncommunicative dickhead butt-face.

The reminder of my poor taste in men makes me roll my shoulders back and lift my chin, determined not to get in too deep with any of the vampires in this castle, even the ones I call friends.

Willpower ramped up to full strength, I push open the door of the building to enter a brightly lit hallway lined with teal tables topped with bouquets of pink wild roses and green herbs. It's the most beautiful entryway I've ever seen—the paintings on the walls are clearly originals, heart-lifting Pacific Northwest landscapes that showcase the region's natural beauty—and the flowers smell so delicious I can't resist leaning in to draw the sweet scent of them into my soul.

Heaven. Pure heaven.

My pulse slows, and a lazy smile tugs at my lips even as my synapses begin to dance, and my feet grow light on the carpet. I can't draw a decent picture to save my life, but art always makes me want to dance, as if that creative energy spills off the canvas into my arms, my legs, all the way down to the tips of my toes.

Inspired, I twirl away from the bouquet in a series of chaîné turns, not realizing I'm being watched until a familiar voice creaks, "Chin up, relax your tongue, and keep that spot steady. If you want to bring home gold, there's no time for sloppy turns, Eliza."

I turn to see Jacque, my dance guru, standing by an open door farther down the hall, his wrinkled hand propped on his narrow hip and Rourke grinning behind him.

"Surprise," Rourke says. "Since you couldn't make it to practice, I arranged for practice to come to you."

"You're the best," I breathe, beaming at them. I dash

across the carpet, throwing my arms around Jacque and shooting Rourke a smile over his shoulder that I know is too flirty for my own good.

But it's not every day a man gives you what you've been wanting most in the world.

Or maybe second most…

I can think of a few things I'd like more than a coaching session, but since all of those things are dangerous, or off-limits, I will dance. I will dance hard, funneling all this ill-advised passion into something safer than sexy vampire boys with smiles that promise to make giving in to temptation the most fun thing ever.

CHAPTER 10

Two hours later, I'm exhausted, covered in a fine sheen of sweat, and sporting a fresh pointe shoe blister on my right pinkie. I'm also so happy I can't stop smiling. Despite my rough night, rhino complications, and the general chaos that is my life right now, I had an incredible practice.

If I dance like that at the pageant, I'll bring home the title. No doubt in my mind.

"Excellent." Jacque pats my shoulder on his way out to meet the helicopter that will fly him home. Yes, a *helicopter*! For my dance coach. For *me*. It's all so wild and extravagant I still can't quite wrap my head around it. "Soak your feet in Epsom salts tonight, mark through the routine a few times tomorrow for timing, and we'll meet again on Friday."

"Thank you so much, Jacque. I appreciate you coming to meet me all the way out here. Truly. Hopefully, in a week or so, everything will be sorted, and I'll be back in the studio for dress rehearsal."

"Don't rush on my account." Jacque tugs his newsboy cap farther down his forehead with a wink. "Never been able to afford a helicopter tour before. I like the view above it all. Our city's pretty from up there."

"I bet." I lean against the door as Jacque moves down the hall toward the exit, graceful but careful in his old age. "I've never been in a helicopter, but I can imagine."

"We'll have to remedy that." Rourke materializes behind me, emerging from wherever he's been hanging out while Jacque and I were practicing. "But tomorrow night, I think. Tonight we have other plans." He extends his hand. "Leo and I thought you might enjoy dinner in the rose garden."

"I would love dinner in the rose garden," I say, keeping my hands clasped. "But I'm gross and stinky, and I need a shower."

Rourke shakes his head. "You're lovely and smell delicious and you need food. You're starving."

I cross my arms. "How can you tell?"

"That I *can* smell," he says, his panty-melting grin curving back into place. "Low blood sugar has a scent like pennies left out in the rain. I can't remember what it feels like, but I'm sure it's miserable, poor lamb." He winks. "Speaking of lamb, the chef is preparing chops and osso bucco, with a choice of rosemary potatoes or fresh baked bread and roasted spring vegetables on the side."

My stomach rumbles, and Rourke's grin grows positively wolfish.

"See? You're famished. Come, dear 'Liza. Let me feed you. It's all warm and ready, and I hate to wait."

"If you were being bossy about anything but food, I'd put up more of a fight." I take his hand, trying not to notice how good it feels to touch him. "But since you're right and I *am* starving..."

"You're good to me," he says, guiding me down the hall. "Though, I bet I can think of other situations when you wouldn't mind a little bossing around."

I narrow my eyes his way, knowing I shouldn't play along but unable to help myself. "Oh yeah? Like what?"

He shrugs casually. "If you were in danger, for example. Like last night."

I nod, blood heating as he threads his fingers through mine, bringing our palms into intimate contact. "True. Safety comes first."

"Exactly." He opens the door at the end of the hall, and we step out into a cool spring evening tinged pink from the recent sunset and rich with the smell of flowers, freshly turned earth, and a whiff of salt from the ocean far away. "A teacher-student situation is another example. I assume you wouldn't be opposed to me teaching you a few self-defense moves tomorrow, so you'll be ready to defend yourself, just in case?"

"I'd love that." Cursing softly, I glance over my shoulder at the castle, which looks even more elegant and mysterious in the fading light. "Which reminds me. Leo gave me a magic bat, but I left it in my room."

"You won't need it tonight. The most stress you'll encounter at dinner is choosing between maple crème brûlée and chocolate lava cake for dessert."

My stomach rumbles again, but I shake my head. "No. No dessert for me. I've only got two weeks left to lose five pounds."

Rourke stops by the wall surrounding the rose garden, turning to face me. "Why would you want to do something ridiculous like that? You don't need to lose five pounds. You're perfect."

I smile. "Thank you, but the zipper on my competition gown says otherwise."

"Then your zipper is a fool." He shifts so he's in front of me, backing me closer to the rock wall, which is still warm and toasty from the sun. "And you need chocolate. I can feel it. The hunger for something sweet is rolling off of you in waves."

I lift my chin, heart beating faster as Rourke braces his hands on the wall on either side of my face. "That's just normal hunger. For vegetables and protein."

"No, it isn't." He leans in, bringing his lips closer to mine. "I can tell the difference, love. I know what you're hungry for, and I think you should let me make sure you get it. Let me boss you into a big slice of chocolate cake, dear 'Liza."

My breath feathers out as tingles race across my skin. I know I'm playing with fire, but I can't seem to stop my mouth from moving. "What if I'd rather be bossed into something more fun than cake?"

Rourke's eyes darken, and a teasing smile curves his lips. "I haven't eaten dessert in a very long time, love. It would have to be something pretty extraordinary to be more fun than cake..." He tilts his head, angling his lips. "Something sinfully sweet... Beautiful... Irresistible..."

Lips prickling with electricity, I whisper, "You've done a good job of resisting up until now."

"Because I'd been ordered to court your friend,

Princess Pea." He brushes his nose lightly against mine. My pulse races faster, but thank God this kind of excitement doesn't seem likely to send me into a shift. "But from the moment I laid eyes on you, I felt..."

My lashes flutter, and my head spins. Having him so close, warm and smelling of cedar and soap and man, is dizzying, intoxicating. "You felt?"

"Hungry." His left hand leaves the wall, coming to rest on the curve of my hip, setting fire to my body with a single touch. "And hopeful," he adds in a softer voice. "Leo's right. You're sunshine, 'Liza. And I haven't seen the sun in so long. But he's also right about this being bad for you. Me... *Us*..."

I brace my hands on his shoulders, stifling a soft moan at the feel of him—so strong and powerful—beneath his dress shirt. "And Leerie would be furious if she saw us here like this."

"And she might. See us." He moves in until the full length of him is pressed against the full length of me and burning becomes my full-time job. "She should be down to dinner any moment."

"So we should stop," I say.

"Most assuredly," he agrees, his hand sliding down to grip my ass through the thin fabric of my velvet pants. "If only you didn't feel so damned good."

"You, too." I arch into him, pressing my breasts against his chest, loving the contrast of soft against hard. "So good."

"And if I didn't suspect you taste even better than you feel." His forehead presses to mine as he groans. The hunger in the sound makes me feel beautiful and

81

powerful, like a sex goddess instead of a hot mess. "Dear Lord, woman, you're killing me."

I can't remember ever feeling like this—so wanted, so desperately desired. Yes, I've had my share of decent sex, and it's been good or occasionally great. But never mind-blowing. Never reality-shifting, the kind of love-making you see in movies or read about in books.

I've had orgasms, not explosions. I've longed for a lover's touch, but I've never felt as if I'll die if I don't have his hands on me soon.

So soon. Five minutes ago, if possible.

"I want you to touch me," I whisper. "So badly."

"Where do you want me to touch you, beautiful?" He cups my face in his free hand as his fingers dig into my ass, drawing me closer until I can feel the evidence of our mutual hunger pulsing against my belly.

"Everywhere," I say. "Everywhere. Please."

With a moan of surrender, Rourke covers my mouth with his. His tongue slips between my lips, teasing and stroking, igniting a firestorm of awareness unlike anything I've felt in so long. Not since I was a teenager drunk on my first real kiss has locking lips with another person made me feel so dizzy and fizzy and free.

I moan into his mouth, pressing closer as the kiss grows hotter, wilder.

"So sweet," he murmurs, trailing kisses down my throat. My breath catches as he rakes the tips of his newly lengthened fangs against where my pulse races beneath my skin. "You smell so sweet. I want to taste you so fucking badly, love."

"Then taste me," I hear myself saying, so high on hormones that anything that gets me closer to Rourke—

even being his pre-dinner snack—sounds amazing. Perfect, even though I've never been the type to fantasize about a vampire kiss.

But now, Rourke cups my breast through my shirt, warning, "If I taste you, it's not going to stop there, love. If I taste you, I'm going to take you. Right here, up against this wall, until you come, screaming so loud there's no way we'll avoid discovery."

The thought is terrifying. And exciting. And so tempting I can't help but whisper against his lips, "I want it. I want you. All of you."

Rourke curses softly. "You're going to be the death of me."

"Oh God, yes," I say, gasping into his mouth as his fingers find my nipple through my shirt, rolling the already tight tip. "That feels so good."

I'm clawing at his shoulders, wild and wanton and starved for more of his kiss, his touch, for the feel of his sharp teeth grazing the delicate flesh of my neck, when the first howl cuts through the night.

Instantly, my blood goes cold.

Rourke and I jump apart, turning to see dozens of giant wolves swarming across the great lawn from the direction of the pond. But they're too big and nasty-looking to be normal wolves, which means—

"The Kin Born," I breathe.

"Run," Rourke orders, guiding me behind him as more snarls fill the air. "Get inside the tent hall, lock yourself in one of the offices. Go, Eliza, now!" he shouts, sprinting forward to meet a group of five wolves all gunning hard for our corner of the lawn. He leaps into the air, fangs bared and fist raised, landing a wicked punch that sends the first wolf flying with a yelp of pain.

But before he can draw his arm back again, he's overrun.

The other wolves tackle him, teeth digging into his arms and legs as they drag him to the ground. He disappears beneath a pile of writhing canines, and I taste earth and overripe beets.

My rhino comes out bellowing, a darker, more dangerous sound than I've ever heard from these lips before. But I'm not afraid or embarrassed about this shift. I'm livid, determined to kick ass and take names. Shaking off the scraps of my ruined tracksuit, I bound toward the wolves piled on top of Rourke.

I'm almost there, close enough that I can hear him cussing as he throws punch after vicious punch, sending one wolf flying, only to have another take its place, when Leerie shouts from across the lawn, "Be careful, Eliza! I'm going for help!"

I jerk my head to the right, spotting my friend's red hair in the lamplight and watching her turn to run back toward the castle—thankfully without any Kin Born on her heels. All around the lawn, wolves are fighting vampires, but only Rourke is so seriously outnumbered.

The wolves aren't fighting fair, a fact that makes me see red.

Bright, blinding red.

Everything is hot and blurry around the edges as I charge the wolves on top of Rourke, stomping on any barking, snarling bodies I can reach. And then, as soon as he's on his feet and clearly holding his own, I take the rhino show on the road, charging and bellowing around the lawn, wreaking havoc.

I'm almost to the duck pond, leaving a trail of whimpering canines in my wake, when I spy Leo sprinting around the side of the castle, carrying a sword he's putting to bloody use, decapitating a wolf in the midst of chewing a pretty vampire's arm from her body.

He reaches down, hauling the twitching corpse off of the woman, but before he can help her to her feet, he's mobbed. Five or six wolves—maybe more—converge on him, abandoning other fights to devote their full, murderous intent to killing Leo.

Killing Leo...

My hurt lurches into my throat and sticks there as a shudder rocks my body. I won't let this happen. If they want to hurt Leo, they're going to have to go through me.

Or maybe I'll go through them...

I rush across the lawn, moving so fast the earth trembles beneath my feet, but before I can reach Leo, something goes wrong. I'm not sure what it is at first, only that one second I'm hauling ass, wild and free, and the next there's pressure and heat against the side of my head. It feels like I'm on fire.

Because I am.

On fire.

Holy shit, I'm on fire!

I fall to the ground, attempting a rhino-sized stop, drop, and roll, only to find myself jerking back into my human skin. I slap at the flames by my neck, coughing as the stench of burning hair fills my lungs, then roll onto my side, pressing my head into the damp grass.

Thankfully, I get the fire under control quickly, with what feels like minimal damage—burned hair is bad, but I'll take it over burned skin any day. But before I can make a run for Leo and hope I can convince my rhino to come back out and fight, claws dig into my bare shoulders, knocking me to the ground.

My lungs deflate, crushed flat by the weight of the animal pinning me to the earth, its snapping jaws inches from my neck. I feel its breath hot on my throat and squeeze my eyes shut, bracing for the death chomp.

A beat later, there's more heat, flaming into the air above me, and my attacker yelps in pain. The weight trapping me vanishes, and I roll over to see Jamal standing over me, his third eye smoking and a hand held out to help me up.

I take it, relief turning my bones to gelatinous ooze as he hauls me to my feet.

"We've got to get you out of here, darling. Not safe for humans out here tonight." Jamal tucks my hand into the crook of his arm, hauling me across the lawn toward the castle. "Sorry for your hair, sweetheart. I was aiming for the coward behind you with his teeth bared and missed."

"Leo…we have to help Leo," I pant, my hair the least of my worries.

People are dying. *Leo* could be dying. Or Rourke. He was holding his own when I left him, but I just learned how quickly the tide can change in a fight.

I pull away from Jamal, spinning to search the lawn and garden wall, sweeping my gaze back and forth, searching the men and women still on the grounds. But there's no sign of either Leo or Rourke, and most everyone else is making quick tracks into the castle.

Most of the wolves are gone, too, the last of them racing away down the hill on the other side of the pond or lying still—dead—on the grass.

"They're probably inside, honey," Jamal says, taking my arm again. "And we should join them, in case the Kin Born decide to come back with reinforcements."

I nod, fighting the tears pressing at the backs of my eyes. "Okay, but I feel like they're still here, I..." I shake my head, knowing I sound ridiculous, but somewhere deep in my bones I just *know* that Leo and Rourke aren't in the castle. That they're still on the lawn somewhere, and that at least one of them is hurt, maybe badly.

"Eliza! Eliza, answer me!"

Leo. It's Leo! "Here! I'm here!" I spin toward the sound of his voice, choking on a sob of relief as I see Leo and Rourke emerging from inside the garden walls, a few terrified-looking staff members behind them.

The waiters and a man in a chef's hat hurry toward the castle as my boys run toward me.

And of course they aren't mine, or boys, but that doesn't matter now.

All that matters is that they're alive and safe and whole.

Or mostly whole...

Rourke's shoulder is bleeding badly enough to make my breath catch as he stops beside me, pulling me into a one-armed hug.

"You're hurt," I say, hugging him gently, carefully, even though I want to clasp him tight to my heart and never let go. "We need to get you inside."

"I'm fine. Nothing a feed won't cure," Rourke says as Leo puts his suit coat around my shoulders. I slide my arms into the warm fabric. That I'm just now remembering I'm naked shows how rattled I am.

"Thank you." I squeeze Leo's hand, holding on tight as he turns back toward the castle with a nod to Jamal.

"We'll take her to the infirmary, Jamal," he says. "Check the annex, make sure anyone sheltering in there knows we're clear, and then meet us in the war room."

"Absolutely, majesty." Jamal nods and hurries away as I insist, "I don't need to go to the infirmary, I'm fine."

"You're burned and you could have internal injuries," Leo says. "I insist you see the doctor. No arguments."

And maybe it's that I'm so glad he and Rourke are okay, or maybe it's how good it feels to hold his hand, but I don't put up a fight. I follow him through the cool grass, trying not to look at the corpses of wolves, or think about how close I came to being one of the dead lying on the lawn.

CHAPTER 11

*N*ow that the worst of the danger has passed and I know no vampire or human lives were lost—only half a dozen Kin Born shifters, who brought on their own demise—there's time to worry about more frivolous matters.

Like hair...

Of course, it's still just hair.

It's not a big deal. It will grow back.

In the grand scheme of things, I was very lucky. We all were. The fact that we got away with cuts and bruises and a few chunks of missing hair is a gift. A miracle.

But as I sit wrapped in blankets in an infirmary exam room, gazing at the post-nuclear wasteland on the right side of my head in the mirror above the sink, contemplating the scabs and clumps of unsalvageable blond fuzz, I can't fight the sinking feeling inside. Because that wasn't just hair, it was part of my arsenal, one of my weapons in the battle to win Miss U.S. and start my new life. Without it, I'll probably have to kiss any hope of bagging that prize money goodbye.

By the time a knock at the door signals the arrival of the doctor, I'm ashamed to say I'm on the verge of tears over the whole stupid thing.

"Come in." I force an upbeat note into my voice and blink faster, willing the waterworks away before I embarrass myself.

"How are you, love?" Rourke. Not the doctor, after all, but I can't say I'm disappointed. I've been dying to see him since we parted ways an hour ago—me to wait with the rest of the only lightly damaged for my turn for attention, and he and Leo to feed, heal, and shore up the shiver's defenses.

"Okay." I glance over my shoulder to see Leo gliding into the room behind Rourke, who looks much improved by an infusion of the red stuff. I meet one intense green gaze and one arctic blue, shivering at the energy they bring into the small space.

"Do you need another blanket?" Leo asks, proving he doesn't miss a beat.

"No, thank you. I'm fine." I *am* fine, but I'm also suddenly very aware of the fact that I'm naked beneath the blanket wrapped around my shoulders, while Leo and Rourke are very clothed. Completely armored up, in fact, in SWAT-type uniforms that prove how serious they are about being prepared for another attack.

I pull the fleece tighter across my body, squeezing my thighs together. "Do you really think they're coming back? Tonight?"

"No," Leo says. "But we're ready if they do."

"Security is on high alert, and everyone knows their

part in keeping the castle secure," Rourke agrees. "Leerie's helping change transfusion bags and stitch up the wounded, so we figured we'd keep you company while you wait for the doc."

"I don't need to see the doctor. Really, I'm fine." I motion toward my savaged head with a shaky smile. "Nothing a bath and a pair of scissors won't cure."

Leo circles the exam table, his stormy expression growing downright menacing as he takes in the remains of my once expertly highlighted and razor-cut pageant hair.

"Good look, right? Probably kick off a new trend at the competition," I say, the quiver in my voice ruining the joke.

"You could have been killed," Leo rumbles. "You should have run the way Rourke told you to."

"I couldn't," I say. "People were in trouble. *You* were in trouble. I had to help."

Leo shakes his head. "You aren't equipped to help. You have zero training or experience in combat situations. You were a liability out there, not an asset."

I sit up straighter. "That's not true! I helped. While I was a rhinoceros, I charged and jabbed at the wolves with my horn and—"

"And caused chaos, making it harder for the guards to get to people who needed help," Leo snaps. "And the second you shifted into your human form, you were completely vulnerable. If the fighting hadn't been largely over by then, you would be dead, Eliza."

"I—" I break off with a sharp exhale, throat going tight. As much as I'd like to deny it, he's right. "I'm sorry."

"Don't be sorry, be smarter," Leo says, his voice rough as he adds, "And bring Pearl with you everywhere you go—to bed, to the bathroom, absolutely everywhere, do you hear me? There's no point in giving you a weapon if you refuse to take it with you."

"I forgot," I say in a small voice, feeling worse with every passing second.

"And if you'd had the bat, I would have gotten to you so much faster," Leo continues, raking a hand through his silky black hair. "It's *my* weapon. I know when it's being used. That's why I chose it for you instead of something smaller and easier to carry."

"I didn't know that, and I really am sorry, Leo. I promise. You have no idea how sorry. When I saw Rourke go down beneath those wolves... And then you.... When I thought you both might die because of me..." I press my lips together and stare at the floor, cursing myself as the white tiles begin to swim before my eyes.

"There, there, we're both fine. And none of this is your fault." Rourke appears at my other side, placing a comforting hand on my back, which makes it harder not to burst into tears. "And Leo isn't mad at you. He's just scared and angry with himself."

"He's right," Leo says, his tone going soft. "I should have made it clear how important it was for you to keep Pearl close at hand. And I shouldn't have let you out of my sight, damn the rules about humans boarding in the shiver wing. It's as much my fault as yours."

"Agreed," Rourke says. "Though I'll take it one step further and say you should have known better than to bring her or Leerie here in the first place, genius."

"As if I had a choice," Leo growls, "I serve at my master's pleasure, Rourke. Not all of us are lucky enough to come from a shiver that celebrates free will. What Gloria wants, Gloria gets, and arguing with her is a good way to end up locked in a starvation chamber."

"Well, it's time Gloria got a wake-up call." Rourke crosses his arms. "She needs to open her eyes and realize what a nest of fucking vipers she's gathered to her bosom. This castle might as well be cursed, too, mate. We'd be safer sleeping on the ground outside the Kin Born fortress. At least then we'd know where our enemies were coming from."

I look up, swiping my fist across my cheeks as I glance from one beautiful, angry face to the other. "What do you mean? You think someone from the shiver told the Kin Born I was here?"

"Told them you were here and offered an engraved invitation to come do their worst," Rourke says, his eyes narrowing. "I'm not buying the broken fence excuse for a hot fucking second."

"Me, either," Leo agrees. "Someone knew they were coming. They arranged for the electricity to go out on the fence. They helped our enemies get to Eliza."

"And were happy to risk the lives of their shiver-mates to do it," Rourke agrees.

"That's awful," I murmur, but something about their theory doesn't sit quite right.

I chew my bottom lip as Leo and Rourke mull over who might want me dead, scrolling through a list of suspects whose names have no meaning to me. I've only met a few of the castle's inhabitants, and none of them seemed murdery, not even Sven, though he clearly still finds me repulsive.

But when he brought tea and scones down when I first arrived at the infirmary, he was civil. Even kind if you count discreetly holding his breath and avoiding any direct comments about how terrible I smell.

And from Sven, I have a feeling it does count.

No, there's something else, something we're all missing...

I furrow my brow, replaying the nightmarish events of the evening. The moment the pack of wolves closed in on Rourke and me, trapping us against the wall... The moment Rourke went down in a pile of flashing fangs and claws... When I spotted Leo across the lawn, facing down half a dozen huge wolves, all alone and outrageously outnumbered...

"It wasn't me," I blurt out, interrupting Leo's heated defense of Gloria, who he swears would never endanger a guest she'd offered the shiver's protection and so couldn't be part of the plot to have me killed.

Rourke cocks his head. "What's that?"

"It wasn't me." My pulse picks up as the pieces click even more tightly together. "The wolves didn't attack me. At least not at first. Not until I started putting up a fight. It was you they were after, Rourke. You and Leo."

Leo frowns but doesn't rush to debunk my theory.

"Well, you were a fairly sizeable adversary, love," Rourke says. "I'm sure Leo and I seemed like easier targets at the time."

I shake my head. "But they weren't scared off by my size when they chased me through the park. And by now I'm sure they've realized that I'm not dangerous. I mean, I may be huge when I'm a rhinoceros, but I'm still me. Before tonight, the closest I ever got to brawling was an intense tug of war over a vintage Kate Spade at a going out of business sale."

"But you've got potential." Rourke scrubs a hand across his chin, seeming to consider my words. "With a little training, you'll be able to hold your own with any wolf. Training starts tomorrow, by the way. I don't care what your dance teacher has to say about it. You need to learn to defend yourself."

"And to use Pearl," Leo adds. "I should have insisted that be the first priority today."

"You're right," I agree. "Self-defense just went to the top of my to-do list."

"I think you're right, as well." Leo nods, his lips pressed tight. "The Kin Born likely intended to take you out eventually, but Rourke and I were the primary targets of tonight's attack."

Rourke arches a brow. "You really think so? We both have a reputation for knowing what to do with ourselves in a fight, Leo. They could have simply been trying to neutralize the most serious threats before going after the lab rat they came for." He lifts a hand my way, fingers spread. "No offense intended, love. Just trying to get into their heads."

"None taken," I assure him. "And you could have a point."

"He could, but my gut says you're right, Eliza. We aren't the only vampires in this castle who can hold our own on the battlefield. The focus on Rourke and me to the exclusion of other strategic targets doesn't make sense, not if you were the only reason they were here."

His words send an absurd thrill through me. I mean, I suppose everyone likes to be told they're right, but hearing Leo, a super serious, thinks-things-through type of guy say he thinks I'm on to something makes me feel smarter than I have since I managed to pull a B in college algebra, despite having zero affinity for logic and even less of a knack for numbers. Not that I'm dumb, but a girl doesn't get a lot of chances to use her brain working at an ice cream parlor or sewing the same apron patterns she's been selling for years.

Leo sighs, and the muscle in his jaw knots into a ball again. "Which means this is bigger than a group of extremists."

"Looks like it." Rourke glances toward the door before doing a slow scan of the ceiling.

"No cameras in here that I know of," Leo says softly, "but we'll have to be careful in the rest of the castle. I'll tell Leerie to gather their things and for her and Eliza to meet us in the garage just before sunrise. I doubt anyone will expect us to leave so soon. If we're quiet, careful, and lucky, we can get away before they try again."

"Before someone here tries to kill you again?" I whisper, clutching the blanket so tightly my knuckles begin to ache. "We shouldn't wait, Leo. We should leave now. Right now. I'll text Leerie and—"

"No." Leo gives my upper arm a squeeze through the soft fleece. "If we go now, someone will stop us. Or follow us. A discreet exit is our best chance. Don't be afraid. We won't let anyone hurt you."

"It's not me I'm worried about." I squirm a hand out

of my blanket cocoon, resting it on Leo's chest. "How can I help? I want to keep you safe, too."

His expression softens, giving me a glimpse of how beautiful he must look when he's relaxed and happy. I've rarely seen Leo in either of those states. He's always got his chin up, soldiering on, soberly fulfilling his duties to his people, even if it means lobbying for a marriage to a woman he doesn't love.

He doesn't love Leerie. I've known that for a while. And after learning what happened to his wife, I doubt he'll ever love anyone again. Marriage probably sounds like a prison sentence to him, but he's still willing to sacrifice his own happiness to bring the gift of the Kiss back to his shiver.

And someone in that shiver is willing to eliminate him for it. To *murder* him, for the sin of having more status or power or whatever insanity motivated tonight's assassination attempt.

I nod. "Seriously. Tell me. If you need me to bust a rhino-sized hole in the castle wall or some asshole vamp's face, I've got you covered."

Leo cups my cheek, sending a flicker of awareness dancing through me before his hand falls away. "Thank you, but no hole-busting needed yet." He turns to Rourke. "For now, we go about business as usual and try not to arouse suspicion."

"Got it," Rourke says. "I'll stay with Eliza until she's seen the doctor and walk her up to bed."

Leo nods. "Perfect. I'll coordinate with Leerie and ask how adept she is with a stick shift, as we'll have to ride in the trunk to avoid sun exposure."

"Not at all adept," I offer, having ridden with Leerie

often enough to know I don't care to do it ever again. "She's not great with an automatic, either. She failed the driving portion of the test three times and is still rocking a learner's permit. I, on the other hand, am an excellent driver." I sniff as I lift my nose higher in the air. "I mean, not to brag, but I am. That's just a fact. I know how to handle machines."

Leo's lips curve. "Then how do you feel about being our getaway driver?"

"I feel good about it," I say, returning his smile. "I may have some elaborate fantasies involving being a getaway driver slash international woman of mystery, in fact."

"Then prepare for those fantasies to become a reality, darlin'," Rourke says, his eyes flashing. "And please tell me you like to go fast."

"Oh yes, I very much like to go fast," I say, cheeks heating as Rourke murmurs, "I thought you might," in response.

Leo clears his throat. "Then I'll—"

He's cut off by a knock at the door. A beat later, a freckle-faced woman with brown braids, looking way too young and wholesome to be either a doctor or a vampire, pops her head in. "Eliza?" She pauses, blinking as she takes in my tall, dangerous, and delicious company. "I'm sorry, I didn't realize you were in here, Prince Leo. Prince Rourke. If you need more time with the patient, I can swing back in a few minutes."

"No, stay," Leo says, his attention drifting my way as he adds, "And take good care of her for us, Nan."

"Always," the doctor assures him warmly. She bustles in, and Rourke and Leo move toward the door,

Rourke promising to wait outside to walk me to my room. But even when they're both out of sight, I don't feel alone.

Because he said "us."

Leo asked the doctor to take good care of me for "us." For him and Rourke. It probably means nothing— just a slip of the tongue—but it makes me absurdly, ridiculously happy. So happy I forget about my awful hair and the danger lurking around every corner, and bask in the glow of being cared about.

CHAPTER 12

a half hour later, I'm escorted to my room by Rourke, with Sven close on our heels. My butler nemesis is still being civil and carrying an armful of garment bags filled with designer dresses the master had sent over as a "sorry you were almost killed while a guest in my castle" present.

"She wants you to take as many as you like," Sven says, his nostrils flaring as he sweeps past me into the bedroom to hang the bags in the walk-in closet. "But pay special attention to what you might like to wear to the party."

"The party?" I ask as Rourke frowns.

"That's still on?" His frown deepens as Sven calls out from the depths of the closet, "It's her anniversary party, Prince Rourke, and you know Master Gloria. Never one to let a little controversy ruin the fun."

"Attempted murder is a 'little' controversy?" I whisper for Rourke's ears only. He arches a brow in agreement, but is all smiles when Sven emerges with my dirty laundry bag in tow.

"I'll just get these washed up," he says, holding the bag at arm's length, pinched between two fingers.

If he were a normal butler, I would insist there's no reason to do my laundry—I've only dirtied one outfit and a pair of pajamas, and I have enough borrowed clothes hanging in the closet to keep me in a different outfit for the next two weeks—but Sven isn't normal. Sven is a pain in my ass with a seriously whacked out nose and a petty part of me enjoys knowing he'll be forced to interact with my dirty clothes, only to learn I've disappeared long before they're ready to be folded.

"See you tonight." Rourke squeezes my hand before trailing Sven to the door. "I hope you sleep well."

"You too," I say, forcing a smile.

I was secretly hoping Rourke might decide to stay a while and see if kissing each other indoors is as amazing as making out by the garden gate, but wretched Sven is watching and I'm sure Rourke has things he needs to do to prepare for our prison break.

That's what the castle feels like now. The magic has gone out of the Strife shiver's headquarters, and I for one can't wait to have its turrets in my rearview mirror.

After Rourke and Sven are gone, I dig around in the closet, finding a roomy designer shoulder bag with more than enough space for toiletries and a few changes of clothes. I pack quickly, take an even quicker shower— swiftly washing what's left of my hair, grateful for the magical vampire salve Nan applied to my scalp to soothe away my minor burns—and find myself flopped on the chaise in the sitting area, already dressed and ready to ride with a good hour to kill.

I've been forbidden from sneaking across to Leerie's room—Leo insisted we should pretend we're settling into bed for the day along with the rest of the house—but he didn't say anything about texting…

Grabbing my phone, I pull up my roomie thread, desperate to know how Leerie's night went and if she's wishing she'd never met my unlucky in love, DNA-scrambled, rhino-charging self.

Eliza: Hey babes, how are you? Hanging in there? I'm so sorry I put you in danger, and I'm so glad you weren't hurt. I never would have forgiven myself if something had happened to you.

Leerie: Don't be silly, honey. The attack wasn't your fault. None of this is your fault. There's clearly more afoot here than anyone realized.

Eliza: Yeah. I'm glad we're leaving.

Leerie: Me too. I'm sure he's very nice, but Jamal's fiery eyeball gives me the heebie-jeebies.

Eliza: Really? I like Jamal. It's Sven who drives me up the wall. He keeps acting like I stink like a homeless man's ass.

Leerie: Oh, he's just old and fussy. Don't take it personally.

Eliza: So I don't reek?

Leerie: Of course not, LOL! I would tell you if you stank, woman. I'm not about to let my girl go wandering around kissing handsome vampires while she smells like Eau de Hobo Bottom.

Eliza: Rourke told you?

Leerie: No, I saw you by the garden. I was on my way over to remind Rourke of his promise to keep his hands to himself when the wolves showed up.

Eliza: Right. Um. So...what if I've decided maybe I don't want him to keep his hands to himself?

Leerie: Um, then you're crazy? You really want two vampire boyfriends? Two vampire boyfriends who are going to want to be a lot more than your boyfriends before too long? They're cursed, Eliza, and under the gun to lock down a mate. They don't have the luxury of taking things slow, and the last time I checked, you were one of the most commitment-phobic people I've ever met.

Eliza: I know, I know. You're right. It's crazy, but...

Leerie: But what?

Eliza: It was the best kiss of my entire life. And if I'm honest, I never wanted to be "just friends" with either one of them, Leerie. We ended up friends because they were after you, but if we'd met under different circumstances…

Leerie: Under different circumstances, they would never have known you exist, Eliza. You don't go to vampire clubs or hang out in supernatural circles. If you didn't have the misfortune of being my roommate, Leo and Rourke wouldn't even know your name, let alone have their fangs set on you. You'd be safe, and I wouldn't feel like the worst friend in the entire world. Goddess, this is all my fault!

Eliza: Stop it! Nothing is your fault. You know better. You're the one who's always saying that the vagina wants what it wants, right? Attraction doesn't always make sense or play by the rules, and it certainly isn't anyone's fault.

Leerie: But this isn't harmless attraction, Eliza. This is the first step down a dangerous path. Get too far down that road and there will be no turning back. You can't just break up with a vampire. It doesn't work that way. There is no vamp divorce. Once you're married, you're married. FOR. EV. ER. No take-backsies.

Eliza: Easy there, no one's talking about getting married. It was just a kiss and a few not-so-innocent thoughts about what it might be like to do more than kiss. That's all.

Leerie: It wasn't just a kiss. It was you staying to fight

when you should have run for cover. It was you risking your life for Rourke and Leo's.

Eliza: They're my friends. I would have done the same for you.

Leerie: Because you love me.

Eliza: Well, yes, of course I do. But I don't... At least I don't think I...
Oh God, do I? Maybe?

Leerie: Love has a way of sneaking in when you're not looking for it, pumpkin. Especially with sweet, smart, loyal, brave, drop-dead sexy men who are allegedly every bit as dangerous in the bedroom as they are on the battlefield.

Eliza: What are they going to do? Murder my vagina?

Leerie: Worse, they'll murder your resistance and sense of self-preservation. Before you know it, they'll have you begging to sign over your life to them like a good little vampire bride. The best thing you can do now is to remove yourself from temptation before the temptation becomes too great. We'll stay with the boys until we're sure they're safe, but then you and I should get the hell out of Dodge. I've already booked tickets on a flight to Germany this afternoon. You can come home with me, meet my terrifying mother, realize your terrifying mother isn't all that bad in the grand scheme of things, rest and recuperate and bang a few hot fairy men so gorgeous they'll make you forget all about Rourke and Leo, and we'll come back to Seattle when things have calmed down.

Eliza: And what if I go rhino on the plane?

Leerie: You won't go rhino on the plane. You'll have Pearl there to help you maintain control. Leo won't mind if you borrow it.

Eliza: The airline isn't going to let me carry a baseball bat onto a commercial flight, Leerie. And if I shift, I could kill everyone on board, send the plane crashing into the ocean, never to be seen again.

Leerie: Then we'll charter a private plane where Pearl will be welcome. It might take a little more time, but I have money saved up for an emergency like this. I'll make it work.

Eliza: No, mama. I can't risk your safety like that. Pearl hasn't been put to the test in a real-life fight-or-flight situation. I have no idea if she'll keep me from shifting. Until I'm me again, I can't risk getting too far off the ground. And I don't want to leave Rourke and Leo. Someone tried to take them both out. They need our help.

Leerie: I know. Leo filled me in. I want to help them, too, but I also want to keep you from making a potentially life-ruining or even life-ending mistake. And I have to go to Germany, whether I like it or not. Right after you left my room this afternoon, I got a call from the high chancellor. My mother's sick.

Eliza: Oh God... I'm so sorry, Leerie.

Leerie: Me too. I'm sure she's going to be fine—she's the strongest person I've ever met—but until she is, as her heir, I'm required to be in court. There's no talking my way out of it this time. Either I take myself there of my own free will, or they'll send someone to drag me there kicking and screaming.

Eliza: Of course you have to go! I know your mother can be a monster, but she's still your mother. If she were to pass and you weren't there to say goodbye...

Leerie: I've already said goodbye. The woman I thought I knew, the one I loved as a child, is dead. If Lenore was ever that person to begin with. If I had a choice, I'd stay here until I was sure you're safe. You're my only real family, Eliza. You and those stupid assholes who want to take you away from me. Even Leo is letting me down. He swore to me he'd never endanger a human woman again, but I've seen the way he looks at you.

Eliza: Really? I feel like he's been mad at me since we left the house yesterday.

Leerie: He's just worried. And scared. When nothing was ever going to come of it, it was okay for him to have a secret crush on you. But now that things have changed, he's realizing how deeply he's fucked up.

Putting you on Gloria's radar, getting you sucked into a world you aren't even a little bit prepared to navigate without getting killed... He's running scared, trying to stuff all the toothpaste back in the tube, but that's not the way love works. Or toothpaste.

Eliza: Or string cheese. Did you ever eat that when you were a kid? That gross cheese that came in a can?

Leerie: God, no. My mother would have had a fit if I put anything that vile close to my mouth, let alone ingested it. I wasn't even allowed to have refined sugar until I was nearly sixty.

Eliza: Fairy adolescence lasts way too long.

Leerie: You're telling me. Back home, I'm still not considered completely grown up. Mark my words, my Aunt Sylphie will try to put me in the children's wing, in one of the rooms with a night nanny outside the door, just in case.

Eliza: In case of what? LOL. In case you need your diaper changed?

Leerie: In case I get hungry in the night and want someone to bring me some porridge. Or my blankets are too warm and need to be swapped out for the summer linens. Or if I have a nightmare and need a cuddle and a night lamp lit.

Eliza: That actually sounds pretty nice. I'd like some porridge and a cuddle.

Leerie: If you come with me, I'll share mine. Come on, Eliza. We can make the flight work, and once we touch down, you'll be safe. No one fucks with my family on their home turf. No one even knows for sure where our home turf is. You won't have to worry about Kin Born attacks or dangerously sexy vampires or betrayal by vagina, and I might even be able to fix the rhino thing. My magic is stronger inside Fairy, and I've always had an affinity for animals as well as plants.

Eliza: I have to go with Leo and Rourke, Leerie. They might not admit it, but they need me. They need someone to watch their back as much as I need someone to watch mine.

Leerie: Then you all better keep each other safe until I get back. Oh, and don't tell the boys you're dropping me off on the way to wherever we're supposed to be going this morning. They'll try to talk me out of it, and that would be a waste of everyone's time. There are certain things you can't say no to, and a summons from the Fey Court is one of them.

Eliza: Okay. But I want you to call me when you get home. As soon as you can. I want to know you made it safely and that everything's all right, and to hear all about your nanny and what kind of porridge she's whipped up for you.

Leerie: Will do. Looks like we're only about ten minutes from go time. Are you packed?

Eliza: I am. Meet you at the end of the hall at five fifty sharp?

Leerie: See you there. And don't forget Pearl.

Eliza: Oh, I won't. Until all this madness is over, Pearl and I are going to be tight. Real tight.

CHAPTER 13

At ten 'til six on the dot, Leerie and I meet up in the soft gloom at the end of the hall. I jab a thumb toward the servant's stairwell, and she nods, confirming my hunch that we should avoid the elevators. Rourke and Leo didn't say how we should get down to the garage, just that we should get there, but the hum of the elevator moving from our floor down to the subbasement seems like the kind of thing that could attract the wrong kind of attention.

And running into one of the servants probably isn't as big a deal as running into one of the shiver members. Though I'd be happy to avoid another run-in with Sven before I leave.

In fact, if I never see Sven again, that would be just fine with me.

"Someone should fire Sven," I whisper as Leerie and I circle down, down, past floors of sleeping human guests to the ground floor and the secret reaches beyond. I'm not sure what's between the ground floor and Subbasement Three, where the cars are parked, but it sure is quiet out there. And dark. If it weren't for the soft blue lights set above the door on each floor, Leerie and I would be running blind.

"You can give him a firm talking to when you're his prince's mate," Leerie hisses back.

I wrinkle my nose. "For someone who doesn't want me to end up vampire-married, you sure do talk about it a lot."

Leerie's lips curve. "Reverse psychology. If I talk about it enough, you'll decide doing it won't be any fun. You know you hate being told what to do."

"It's not your favorite thing, either," I remind her. "That's the only reason you didn't marry them yourself, right? Because too many people told you it would be a great idea."

"No, I'm not married to them because I don't care about Rourke or Leo in that way. And because I could tell that you did."

The confession makes me stumble on the final step down to the bottom landing.

Leerie pauses with her hand on the door leading into to Subbasement Three to pin me with a sober look. "It's all right if you can't resist the pull, Eliza. There's more than a whiff of destiny lingering around you three. Yes, if you choose a life with Leo and Rourke, I'll be worried about you. But I'll also be happy for you. As long as you're happy, *I'm* happy. I want you to know that. Just in case we don't see each other again."

My heart skips a beat. "Why wouldn't we see each other again, Leerie? What aren't you telling me? Is your mom really dying? Are they going to hold you prisoner and force you to be the queen of the fairies? Do you need me to fly over and bust you out as soon as I'm human full time and can be trusted on a plane?"

Her lips curve in a sad smile. "I appreciate the offer, but no. If I stay, it will be my choice. For all my complaining and running away, I love my people. And if I don't stay and foster order, someone else will sweep in and create chaos. I can't let that happen, not when my parents worked so hard to make Fairy a place that decent creatures could be proud to call home again."

I lean in, hugging her tight. "But we won't say good-bye. We'll see each other soon. I can feel it in my gut, and you know my gut never lies."

Leerie folds me up in her much longer arms. "I hope you're right. I'm not ready to let go of you yet, sister. I need more tea in the kitchen and all-night holiday parties and dancing naked under the full moon."

"You naked weirdo," I say, sniff-laughing. "We're dancing in clothes next time. Swimsuits, at the very least."

Someone clears his throat softly above us, and Leerie and I draw apart, turning to see Rourke and Leo on the landing, their own bags clutched in their hands.

"We should go," Leo says. "Sunrise is in less than an hour. The human servants will be arriving for their shifts soon. Best for us if none of them see anything they'll be able to report to the master when she wakes."

I nod. "All right. We're ready."

Or as ready as we'll ever be, anyway...

CHAPTER 14

*L*eerie throws open the door to the parking garage, and she and I both suck in a horrified breath.

"Oh, for goddess's sake," she hisses, bouncing from foot to foot with her arms hugged tight around herself.

I instantly begin to shiver hard enough to make my teeth clack together. "D-damn. What are you vampires doing down here? Farming icicles?"

"Storing cars," Leo says, striding into the dimly lit concrete womb and turning right at what looks like a vintage Lamborghini. "Cars don't feel the chill."

"Neither do we," Rourke says with a wink and a circle of his arm. "Come on, ladies. The cameras were off when I left the control room ten minutes ago, but I can't promise how long they'll stay that way."

"Is that a Veneno Roadster?" I whisper to Leerie as we hurry after them, past more high-dollar and highly buffed cars than I've ever seen gathered in one place.

"I think so," she says, eyes narrowing as she peeks down the next row. "And I think that's a Ferrari Mondial. I wrecked one of those in 1984, the first time I tried to get my license."

I blink up at her, stunned. I mean, I knew she was a terrible driver, but, "You've been trying and failing to get your license for almost a hundred years?"

She shrugs. "Yeah. But the first time I tried it was in Mississippi. They have a really hard test."

"In Mississippi," I repeat dubiously.

"What?" Leerie bristles before succumbing to another shiver hard enough to make her curls tremble around her head. "Don't hate on Mississippi. They can't help it. They had that giant rise in population after Louisiana went under in the Meltdown, and they weren't the most well-funded state as far as social programs went in the first place. They're doing the best they can. And so am I. Driving is dumb, anyway."

"Driving is dumb," I agree, even as my heart begins to race as I spot the beauty Leo's clicking open in front of us. "Oh my God, is that..."

"Porsche 911 GT RS," he says, his lips curving as he tosses his duffle bag into the back seat. "I figured your first getaway car should be something you could really take out for a spin."

"And it's got an enchanted speedometer." Rourke chucks his bag in after Leo's, and circles around to the open trunk. "So you can go as fast as your speed demon heart desires."

"Don't tell her that," Leerie says, shivering her way over to the passenger's side. "She's already a maniac, even without magical intervention."

I nod, grinning as Pearl begins to glow in my hand. "Oh yeah. This is going to be fun."

Leo glides in front of me, dropping his voice as he asks, "You'd be shifting right now, wouldn't you? If you didn't have Pearl? That's how excited you are about taking this beauty out for a spin?"

I nod, biting my lip, pulse spiking again as I meet Leo's gaze. "Maybe. Is that bad?"

"No, it's…" He trails off with a shake of his head and a soft sigh.

He doesn't finish the sentence, but I have a pretty good idea what he's thinking. It's there in his flashing eyes, in the tilt of his head, in the way his tongue slips out to dampen his lips.

Leo, the somber and serious, has a wild side after all.

"So you like fast cars, Mr. Poplov?" I tease, handing over my bag when he reaches for it.

"I do, indeed, Ms. Frank." He crosses back to the Porsche, dropping my bag on the back seat before shutting the door and holding out the keys. "Our lives are in your hands. Are you ready?"

"I was born ready." I tuck Pearl under my arm as I take the keys, a sizzle rushing up my arm as my fingers brush Leo's.

"Keep Pearl on your lap," he says, casting a pointed look at the glowing bat. "Just in case. Our destination is already programmed into the GPS."

I salute him with my key-holding hand, loving the jingle they make. "Yes, sir."

"See you on the other side," he says, crawling into the exceptionally roomy trunk beside an already sleepy-looking Rourke.

I peer inside, taking in three pod-like sleeping depressions built into the frame, complete with latches that lock from the inside. "Will there be a safe place to unload you guys when we get there? Or should I leave you locked up until sunset?"

"There's subterranean parking," Rourke says with a yawn, seeming awfully relaxed for a man fleeing an attempt on his life. "Just pull in through the gate, spiral all the way down, and give a knock on the trunk. We'll be out in a wink."

Leo reaches for a handle inside. "You'll be fine. Just don't stop until you're off the property."

"Far off," Rourke adds. "A hundred miles with no tails should do it."

I start shivering again, the heat generated by the getaway car reveal excitement evaporating in the face of the reality of what we're about to do. "And if someone is tailing us?"

"Then lose them," Leo says, shutting the trunk with a firm *thunk*.

"Lose them, right," I mutter, giving Pearl a twirl at my side as I head to the driver's seat. "Here we go, then."

"Saints protect us." Leerie clutches her seatbelt as I arrange Pearl across my lap and slide the key into the ignition, sending the 911 purring to life. "If I pass out, don't try to revive me until you're ready to let me out, okay? I don't want to be awake for this if I don't have to be."

I brace my hand on her seat, gazing over my shoulder as I back out of the parking space. "Right," I whisper, shifting into drive and pulling toward the exit ramp. "Where do you want me to drop you off, by the way? Rourke said not to stop until we're at least a hundred miles away."

"It doesn't matter, really," Leerie says as I guide us up, up, back toward the soon-to-be-rising sun. "Just as long as I'm not too far from the ocean. There are fairy rings all up and down the west coast. Can't walk more than a dozen miles or so without tripping over one if you know where to look. Since we won't be flying together, I won't have to use my plane ticket, and can just travel fairy-ring direct." She sinks lower in her seat, voice dropping as we emerge from the final slope with a dip as we roll out into the gray light of early morning. "Oh goddess, Eliza, there's no way we're getting out of here. There are guards everywhere!"

"It's fine. Just play it cool and follow my lead." I tuck my hair behind my ear, flashing a smile for the guard who holds a hand out, stopping us beside the fountain in the center of the drive. Leo told me not to stop, but my gut insists it's far better to try to talk our way off the property than to go out engine roaring and middle fingers blazing.

"We're on lockdown, miss," the man says, motioning back toward the castle with his serious-looking stun gun. "No one in or out except staff, and all vehicles are searched on entry."

"Of course," I agree, nodding, "but we've got a plane to catch. Prince Leo is sending us away. For our own safety."

The guard frowns. "I haven't heard anything about travel plans. Let me call up to the house."

"Yes, please do," I insist. "Hopefully we can catch

him before he goes to rest. The master is already rest-ing. As you know, she turns in early and gets super not-happy if she's disturbed for anything but a serious emergency. Which this isn't." I shrug. "But that's okay. Prince Leo doesn't get quite as mad as the master. Just a tiny bit grouchy, really. I'm sure he'll understand why you woke him up and bothered him instead of just checking our plane tickets."

The man's thick nose wrinkles before shifting to one side and then the other. He glances over his shoulder again, but the other guards are too far away to ask for help without drawing attention to himself.

"I have the tickets here," Leerie says, tapping at her phone screen. "Just a second, and I'll pull them up. We're going to stay with my family. My mother has an army, you see. Huge army. Famous for skinning people alive in the sixth century, but a lot more civilized now."

"But still dangerous," I add. "Which Prince Leo is super happy about. He knows we'll both be safer there than we'd ever be here. I mean, no offense, you're clearly a great guard, but you're not a thousand years old."

"Or a fairy." Leerie laughs, doing a much better job of playing it cool than I expected. "Or armed with weapons that can slice open skin at twenty paces." She smiles as she holds out her phone, the tickets now visible on the screen. "Did you know that? That fairies have weapons that can gut you before they even touch you? Isn't that wild? I mean, the wonders of the world, am I right?"

"Um, right." The guard's throat works as he casts a cursory glance at the tickets before waving a hand.

"Head on down the hill, ladies, I'll radio ahead that the prince gave you permission to leave."

"Thanks so much!" I sing, reaching for the window button and buzzing it up.

The guard stands only to bend down a beat later, motioning for me to drop the window again. Pulse stuttering, I lower it a crack. "Yes?"

"Though I'm sure he'd want you to have an escort to the airport," the guard says, pulling his walkie-talkie from his belt. "I'll get a couple armored cars sent down. They'll meet you near the exit, and you can all go together."

"Great, thanks for nothing," I say through gritted teeth as I drop the window all the way down.

"What was that?" the man asks, his words turning to a sharp *oomph* as I jab him in the gut with Pearl. There's a flash of light, and he goes flying, sliding across the pavement to tumble heels over head into the fountain with a splash.

"Sorry!" I shout as I put the pedal to the metal, roaring down the hill toward the exit as Leerie squeals softly in the passenger's seat behind me.

"Oh goddess, oh goddess, oh goddess," she chants, hunkering lower and covering her head with her arms.

"It's going to be fine!" I cut left and then right, zooming around a man pushing a heavily loaded flatbed. "I'm a great driver. Nothing to fear but fear itself."

"The tree! The tree!" Leerie squeals as I rumble off the road, avoiding a truck headed up the drive and swerving toward a massive oak near the road while I'm at it.

But I didn't even get *close* to hitting it. Not nearly

as close as I get to hitting the guard who rushes from the woods with his stun gun aimed at the wheels, anyway. But it's good that I almost clip the guard! It sends him diving into a patch of blackberry vines, and we avoid getting shot off the road. I call that a win-win.

"It's fine! We're fine," I shout, pulse thundering in my ears as I barrel closer to the closed and heavily armed gate at the end of the drive, where more guards are lifting guns to their shoulders.

I'm calculating the odds of not getting shot while maintaining enough speed to have a chance of smashing through the extremely solid-looking wrought iron, when the entrance gate miraculously swings open on the other side.

With a whoop of celebration, I skid into the opposite lane and floor it, gunning hard toward the delivery van beginning to pull in from the road.

"Brake! Brake!" Leerie screeches, clinging to the handle above her door. But I don't brake. I speed faster, faster, zipping around the van and cutting the wheel hard to the right.

And yes, the Porsche lifts onto two wheels for a second or two.

And yes, it does sort of feel like flipping over is a possibility there for a moment. But we don't flip. We drop back onto the road and roar away from the castle, leaving the guards to eat our dust.

All in all, I consider it a successful first outing as a getaway car driver. Certainly nothing worth fainting over.

But apparently Leerie would disagree.

"Leerie?" I glance her way to find her slumped against the door. "Leerie, you okay?"

I reach over, brushing her hair from her face to find her eyes closed and her breath coming slow and steady and smile. "Poor thing. You sleep. I've got this."

And I do.

I cut a convoluted trail through the suburbs, ensuring any tail we might have acquired gets lost in the confusion, before heading west to the coast. By the time the temperature starts to drop and the scent of sea spray fills the air, Leerie is coming to.

"Never again," she says with a sigh.

"Aw, come on. You have to ride with me again. How else are you going to get to the grocery store?"

"I'll bike. Walk. Crawl on my hands and knees very slowly. And I'm not just swearing off riding with you. I'm done with cars. Period. Full stop."

I pat her knee. "You'll change your mind. Cars are convenient. And fun."

"You seriously thought that was fun?" She jabs a thumb over her shoulder. "That near-death experience back there?"

"We weren't near death," I scoff. "We were serious-injury adjacent."

Leerie snorts. "Bunch of lunatics. You deserve each other."

"Who deserves each other?"

"Now, let me out," she says, ignoring me. "There. By the little blue house with the green fence."

"Do you know the people who live there?" I ask, slowing on the next curve.

"No one lives there. At least not recently. It's been

empty for several months." She reaches over the seat, grabbing her bag from the back. "I'll be able to hide there until nightfall, when it will be safe to sneak down to the fairy circle by the beach."

"That's still so weird to me." I pull into the drive, carefully avoiding the potholes in the cracked asphalt. "That you can sense a place is vacant without even looking inside the joint."

"Buildings have energy fields, too. If you pay attention, they'll let you know when they've been abandoned."

"I don't know about that, but I know you'd be a really good cat burglar."

"I'll keep that in mind," she says, "in case the interior design thing doesn't work out long-term. Assuming, of course, that I'm allowed back in the human world."

My lips turn down hard. "Don't say that. You're coming back."

Leerie turns to me as I put the car in park. "If I don't, remember, I want you to be happy. Whatever happiness looks like for you, whoever it might or might not involve. You answer to no one but yourself, Eliza. Remember that. And trust your gut—you've got a good one."

Brow furrowing, I nod. "I will. But I don't want to think about my life without you in it, Leer. Come back if you can. And send word soon, okay? I want to know what's going on with you. That you're safe and well and happy and not married to that awful asshole."

She snorts. "Absolutely not. I'll rot in hell before I'll be his wife. And I promise, I will be happy. Not even court politics can get me down, not if I don't let it." Her smile is clearly forced, but when she leans across the seat to hug me, her embrace is as warm as ever. "Take care, darling. Hope to see you soon."

"Soon," I echo as she reaches for the door handle.

"Tell them goodbye for me." She opens the door, pausing before she steps out. "And tell them to be good to you or I will send Unseelie nightmare creatures to peck their eyes out while they sleep."

I smile. "Will do. Love you."

"Love you, too. Now, get out of here. You've still got a long way to go." Leerie slips out of the car and jogs around to the back of the abandoned cottage. I wait until she disappears—presumably to pick the lock on the back door and haunt a stranger's house for the rest of the day—and blow her a kiss for good luck.

Then I pull back onto the road, headed north with two vampires in my trunk, wondering how on earth this came to be my life.

And why I'm enjoying it so much.

"Sick in the head," I mutter, fighting a smile as I lay on the gas. "Clearly sick in the head."

But as I zoom around the next curve a little too fast, I don't feel sick. I feel awake, alive, and part of something I'm not sure I want to end.

At least, not anytime soon.

CHAPTER 15

Two hours north of where I left Leerie, I reach the turn for the village of Port Bailey and veer east, along what's left of this part of the coast. Decades before I was born, the polar ice caps shrank to a fraction of their previous size, flooding the world's coastlines and submerging entire cities—sometimes entire states or countries. Dozens of island nations simply disappeared, their citizens relocated as refugees or, if they refused to leave, abandoned to their fate.

Every Halloween, the internet explodes with creepy lists—"Top 5 Dive-Worthy Ghost Cities" or "7 Most Famous Lost Civilizations"—the tragedy reduced to click bait for a few days while everyone is in the mood to be scared.

"No more scary stuff," I whisper as I guide my sleek machine up to the hamlet perched on the edge of a cliff.

I've had my fill of scary, thank you very much. I'll take cozy and boring any day, and thankfully, it looks like Port Bailey is going to deliver.

Main Street has two stoplights—one in front of a quaint clapboard hardware store peddling fishing lures and walking sticks on its wide front porch, and one by an adorable, weathered library where a class of preschoolers is having story time under a blossoming cherry tree. The hamlet is the picture of sweetness and light, complete with charming shops, a fish shack, a Farmer's Table Co-op grocery, and an old lighthouse someone has meticulously restored near the edge of town.

I've got my eye on that lighthouse from the moment I cruise in. When it becomes clear that the white and blue beauty is my final destination, it's all I can do not to squeal with delight.

But Leo and Rourke are probably asleep back there, and I don't want to wake them. Or scare them if they're awake and listening to what's going on in the outside world.

As I swing into the driveway, the electric gate opens automatically, and I pull inside, steering around to the back and into the deceptively normal-looking garage beneath the structure. But it's not an ordinary garage, of course. It's the entrance to another spiral into the earth. This one only goes down about thirty feet, however, before it dead-ends in a spacious parking area, big enough to fit four or five vehicles.

Since we're the only ones here, I pull in diagonally across three spaces, just for the thrill of it—breaking the rules can be fun, even when there's no one around to enforce them—and hop out, stretching my arms over-head, wincing at the cracking sound from near the base of my spine.

I'm about to circle around to tap on the trunk when it pops open on its own and Leo emerges in one graceful swoop. He runs a hand through his not-at-all mussed hair as he arches a brow my way. "You two planned that, didn't you? To send Leerie home while Rourke and I were trapped back here, unable to talk sense into her?"

I bare my teeth in a guilty smile-grimace. "Yeah. She insisted. I'm sorry. She said there was no point in talking. She had to go. Fairy law and all that."

"Laws were meant to be broken." Rourke climbs out more slowly, pausing to stretch his neck before slamming the trunk closed. "Look at us. We've broken at least three major vampire laws since this morning."

Chest squeezing tight, I look back to Leo. "Is that true? I didn't hurt anyone on the way out of the compound, by the way. Just knocked one guard into a fountain, one into a blackberry bush, and maybe ran a delivery van off the road. Didn't even have to bust through a gate, which was good because I'm pretty sure you'd need a tank to get through that sucker."

"All good to hear," Leo says. "But Rourke is still correct. We disobeyed a direct order from both of our masters and taken ourselves out of play while our shivers are on high alert. But none of that can be helped, so..." He lifts a shoulder and lets it fall, seemingly unconcerned.

"Aren't you going to get in big trouble?" I ask. "Don't vampires still torture each other and...stuff like that?"

Rourke grins, his dimple popping as he comes to stand beside me and reaches out to pinch my chin. "Look at that. She's worried about us, Leo. Don't fret, sweetheart, Leo and I have been starved and beaten before. Nothing we can't handle and come out on the other side full of piss and vinegar. Especially piss." He winces. "I could use a break. Be a love and pop upstairs to make sure the blackout curtains are drawn before Leo and I bring up the luggage?"

"On it." I nod, pressing the keys into Leo's hand before turning and trotting toward the elevator I spotted on the drive in.

I smile to myself on the way up, remembering a time when I assumed vampires didn't do normal things like use the bathroom—or have a heartbeat or a reflection, for that matter. Until Leo and Rourke came into my life, I'd never met a vampire. I only knew the folklore.

I still don't know much—I've always been too shy to ask questions, worried I'll come off like the stupid human I am—but maybe that will change while we're here. Looks like we'll have plenty of time to chat.

The house is gorgeous, but small, without so much as a television or radio for entertainment. I suppose we'll have to play the board games I spot as I'm pulling the living room curtains shut.

Or find other ways of entertaining ourselves…

"Off to a bad start, Eliza," I mutter as I take care of the curtains in the master bedroom and move across the kitchen to the larger, bunk bed filled second bedroom. Less than ten minutes in and I'm already thinking about what it might be like to tumble into one of these beds with Leo.

Or Rourke. Or Leo *and* Rourke.

It doesn't bode well, and my only comfort is that I'm way too tired to get into any trouble today.

By the time I tell Leo and Rourke that the coast is clear, unpack my suitcase in the master bedroom they insist I take, and fix myself a bowl of soup for a late lunch from the pantry's abundant supply of canned foods, I'm so exhausted I can barely keep my eyes open.

The boys aren't looking much better. Rourke is slumped in a chair, and Leo's head hangs wearily between his shoulders as he braces his hands against the island in the kitchen, stretching his calves.

"I have to crash, guys. I'm sorry." I lean against the frame of the door to the bedroom, fighting to hold up the concrete weights that have settled on my lids.

"No need to apologize," Rourke says with a tired smile. "You've been up longer than either of us, and I'm knackered. Being awake during the day is easier than it used to be, but it still hurts a little."

"I'll take first watch while you both get some rest," Leo says.

"Are you sure? There're more than enough beds to go around." Rourke nods toward the larger bedroom, where two twin beds sit side-by-side on one wall and a full-size bunk bed fills the corner. Clearly, this hideout was designed to shelter not only Rourke, but several of his nearest and dearest, as well. "The security system is state of the art, and I've never brought anyone from our world here. It's so far off the radar, not even my master knows my name's on the deed. It should be safe for us all to take a kip."

Leo plants himself in one of the wrought iron stools on the far side of the island, turning his back on the softer, cushier furniture in the living room behind him.

"I'll keep watch for an hour or two. Make sure we weren't followed. Maybe then I'll turn in."

"And maybe flowers will bloom out of my asshole," Rourke says pleasantly. "Suit yourself, Mr. Control Freak." He lifts a hand my way. "See you this evening, love. Sleep well and sweet dreams."

He winks at me, a wicked wink that sends memories of that kiss by the garden flitting through my mind. In all the chaos of last night and the escape from Castle Doom this morning, I haven't had a whole lot of time to think about that kiss.

But I'm thinking about it now.

And so is he, judging by the twinkle in his sea-glass green eyes.

God, that kiss...

It was a kiss to rival all other kisses, such a sweet, sexy experience that a misbehaving voice in my head insists we should make this nap a co-ed affair. But the other voice in my head—the reasonable, not ruled by my libido one—insists this isn't the time or place. That there will *never* be a time or place because Rourke has serious responsibilities and the weight of his shiver's survival on his shoulders and isn't in the market for a "let's have amazing sex and see where things go" kind of relationship.

And then there's Leo. Leo, who probably wouldn't be jealous, per se, but who certainly wouldn't approve of Rourke and I shacking up in the same bed.

Leo, who I would also very much like to kiss...

Leo, who is watching me through hooded eyes, as if he can read every wayward thought flitting through my head.

"Right. Good night. Or good afternoon." I lift a hand, waving at the insanely gorgeous men staring at me as I trip over my own feet and nearly take a tumble while I'm shutting the door between us.

This is a bad idea—me, Leo, and Rourke, all alone in a romantic lighthouse at the edge of the sea with nothing but the sound of crashing waves and a cabinet full of board games to occupy our time. The two of them might be old and wise and capable of exercising restraint, but I'm twenty-eight, not two hundred and eighty. And it's been years since I've had good sex, let alone the supernova of pleasure I have no doubt awaits in any bed with Rourke or Leo in it. Eugene was a proficient, adequate lover at best, and an uninspired one at worst.

"And look how much trouble you got into with him," I mutter to myself as I crawl under the perfectly heavy covers. "Just imagine how badly things could go awry with a gorgeous, sexy, ancient vampire."

I try to scare myself, I really do, but as I drift off to sleep, the visions dancing through my head aren't frightening at all. They're only tempting—wild and wonderful, and just the right amount of wicked.

$\mathcal{I}$ crash hard and sleep like the dead. Or the undead, I suppose—vampires are notoriously hard sleepers—and wake feeling refreshed but disoriented.

Is it still daytime? Nighttime?

Today, tomorrow, yesterday?

I have no idea.

"Pretty sure it isn't yesterday. Unless we've entered a time vortex," I say, rolling out of the giant bed. I use the bathroom, wash my hands, and brush my teeth, doing my best not to look at the nightmare that is the right side of my head.

"Don't do it," I mutter to my reflection. "Just don't. Looking only makes it worse."

"Everything all right in there?" a voice from outside the door asks, making me yip, jump, and bang my knee on the cabinet.

"Sorry. Didn't mean to scare you," he adds. "Just wanted to make sure you had everything you need."

Leo.

I limp to the door and open it with a laugh. "No worries. And yes, everything is great. Just talking to myself."

"Makes sense. You're good company," he says with a nervous-looking smile.

Leo? Nervous? What madness could have caused this state of affairs?

"Thanks." I run a hand over the good side of my head, smoothing my sleep-fuzzed hair. "What's up?"

"I was thinking. While I was on lookout. About..." He motions toward my head, still so adorably awkward I can't help but smile, though my hideousness isn't really funny.

"Yeah. I know where it is," I tease. "It's okay. It'll grow back."

"But your contest is in less than two weeks. And I know you're supposed to look a certain way. So I thought..." He pulls one hand from behind his back and holds up his cell. On the screen is a picture of a beautiful, edgy-looking model with one side of her head shaved and the other fluffed into outrageous 1980s-style curls. "Maybe something this?"

I gingerly take the phone, so touched I can't speak for a moment. When I do manage to get words out, they're husky, "I love it. It's perfect. Pretty and punk, but not too much for Miss U.S." I look up at him, smiling so hard my cheeks hurt. "Thank you, Leo. So much. You can't imagine how much better this makes me feel. I can't wait to get to a hair salon."

He withdraws his other hidden hand, revealing a trimmer. "I could do it for you. I used to cut my men's hair. When we were occupying Manchuria after the war. Want me to see what I can do?"

Self-consciously, my hand drifts to my head, fingertips brushing over the sad clumps left behind. It's so awful there's no way Leo could make it any worse, and how could I possibly say no to such a thoughtful offer? Even if he messes up and I have to get my stylist to fix it later, it will be worth it to show him how grateful I am for his good heart.

And his respect.

The fact that he hasn't tried to pressure me into taking his money again hasn't escaped my attention. Or my gratitude. It's nice to feel respected by your friends, even when you know your decisions don't make sense to them.

"Let's do it." I nod, emotion tightening my throat. "But maybe I should wash it again first? I think I got all the blood out when I showered this morning, but I was anxious about driving the getaway car. I could have missed a spot."

"Why don't you come into the kitchen and let me wash it for you at the sink?" Leo nods over his shoulder. "I've already set out shampoo and conditioner."

"Oh no, you don't have to do that," I say, my cheeks heating at the thought. "I can just jump in the shower."

"I know I don't have to," he says, leaning against the doorframe. "I'd like to. To thank you for your excellent getaway driving. And to apologize for putting your hair and your head in danger in the first place." He rolls a lazy shoulder. "And to make Rourke miserably jealous while I'm at it. While we were locked in the trunk, he made sure to mention about a hundred times the fact that he kissed you."

A surprised laugh bursts from my lips, and my blood begins to fizz the way it did when Leo touched my face in the armory. "I didn't think you guys were the jealous type."

"We aren't," Leo says. "But we do enjoy tormenting each other, challenging each other. Playing aggressive games of tag football, beating each other at cards, bragging about who might have kissed a beautiful woman first..."

First. That one little word is enough to make butterflies dance in my vagina.

I worm my hands into the front pocket of my gray sweatshirt, the better to keep them to myself. "So the hair-washing would just be a way to get back at Rourke?" I peer at Leo from the corners of my eyes. "Your 'no fragile humans' policy is still in effect?"

"Of course it," he says, the sober note in his voice at odds with the heat flickering in his gaze. "But just because I'm determined never to put another hair on your head in danger doesn't mean flirting has to be off-limits."

I arch a brow. "Flirting? You? Mr. Serious? Do you even know how?"

"I used to," he says with a twitch of his lips, "but it's possible I've forgotten. It would probably be wise if I gave it another try, before the skill atrophies and falls off. Like a bloodless limb."

I laugh. I can't help it.

"No good?" he asks, playing dumb. "I shouldn't

mention bloodless limbs while trying to woo a woman to my sink?"

"No. Bloodless limbs are a hard pass." I press my lips together, but there's no shutting down my smile. "But I will accompany you to your sink, sir. We can't let Rourke get away with tormenting you while you couldn't escape him."

"Good." The pleasure in Leo's eyes makes the fizzing even worse, until I'm all bubbles inside. "Then we can go out onto the deck for the cut. It's a beautiful evening. There's still some sunset glow left in the clouds."

"That sounds lovely. And this is very sweet of you. I appreciate it."

"I appreciate your understanding." He leads the way across the bedroom and out into the quiet kitchen. Judging by the closed door on the other side of the apartment, Rourke is still down for the count. "I'm sorry about all of this. We were supposed to be protecting you, and somehow our roles became reversed."

"We'll just have to protect each other, then," I say as he turns on the water, holding two fingers in the stream to adjust the temperature. "That's what friends do, right?"

He glances over his shoulder, an inscrutable expression on his face.

"Right?" I prod. "Because we're friends? Who might flirt a little, just to help you remember how to get girls?"

He blinks. "Right. Sorry. Of course. I was just thinking."

"About what?"

"Friendship. Honor. Betrayal. Who might have the most to gain from pretending to be a friend and then betraying my trust."

I pucker my lips. "So just the easy, light-hearted stuff, then?"

He smiles, big and bright, and my heart does spinning, squeezing things. Things that assure me I don't want to help Leo get other girls.

But I won't think about that now. After all, there aren't many women in the village, Leo can't go out during the day, and Port Bailey doesn't look like a hotbed for nightlife.

Good luck finding anyone else to practice flirting with, buddy. You're mine for now, I think, beaming back at him.

"And what are you thinking?" he asks, his eyes narrowing.

"That you have a gorgeous smile," I say, choosing the safest version of the truth. "You should bring it out for show-and-tell more often."

His nods. "Maybe I will. As soon as I figure out who's trying to kill us. Now get your head under my spray and let me take care of you."

"Sounds kind of dirty when you put it that way," I say, enjoying the freedom to flirt every bit as much as I thought I would.

Leo grunts, but he's still smiling as he shakes his head. "Not dirty. Clean. I'm going to get you all cleaned up and ready to do battle, Ms. Frank. Those judges aren't going to know what to do with you."

"Except give me first." I slide in front of him, keenly aware of his large body angling in behind me.

"Exactly," he murmurs, his hand resting on the small

of my back. My nerve endings sizzle as he adds, "Now flip over. Head in the spray."

"Yes, sir." I slowly bend forward, letting my hair spill over in a tumble of gold, hoping the effect is still at least a little sexy. Leo is standing on my left side, not my right, after all, and from the left I'm still 100 percent beauty queen.

"I'm going to regret this, aren't I?" His fingers brush across my bare neck, smoothing loose strands into the water.

"Regret what?" I ask, my eyelids fluttering closed as my nipples pull tight inside my bra. Who knew that such a relatively innocent skin-on-skin moment could do this? Could make my body ache and my knees go weak? Could make my stomach triple backflip as Leo guides the spray from one side of my scalp to the other?

"Opening this door with you," he says, angling farther behind me until his pelvis brushes lightly against my ass and we're in such a blatantly sexual position my heart begins to beat between my legs. I sway my hips subtly left, then right, left then right, seeking friction, but the brush of my thighs against each other isn't nearly enough.

Finally, after a beat, Leo says, "Stop it, Eliza."

"Stop what?" I ask, unable to resist one more wiggle or the giddy grin that spreads across my face when Leo curses softly in response.

"That," he says. "Do you enjoy torturing me?"

"The torture goes both ways," I say, my voice breathy, "believe me."

"Is that so?" Leo's hand skims from my waist to my ribs, his fingertips so close to my breast that my nipples sting with wanting. "Bend over a little more. I can't reach the back."

I obey, breath catching as my bottom makes contact with where he's definitely not unhappy to see me. He's not hard, but he's getting there, and when we touch, he doesn't pull away. He presses closer, and my head spins so fast I have to brace my hands on either side of the sink to keep from sagging to the floor.

"You're a bad man." I moan as he massages lavender-scented shampoo into my hair, his deft fingers treating my still tender scalp with exquisite care. "I can't believe I thought you were the nice one."

"I *am* the nice one." Leo's hips shift forward, making me moan again as the thicker, harder length of him presses against me. "But if the torture really is to go both ways, I have to hold up my end of the bargain. Close your eyes. I'm going to rinse."

"My eyes are closed," I say, shivering as his fingers rub the shampoo from my skin.

"Cold? Should I adjust the temperature?"

"It has nothing to do with the temperature, and you know it." I reach back, running my hand down the side of his hip to grip his thick quad muscle through his suit pants, a surge of triumph surging through me when he growls in response.

He slicks conditioner onto my head, combing it through the strands with a confidence that has me imagining what it would be like to have his fist in my hair, pulling my head back as he—

Nope. *Not* going to think that. If I let my thoughts go that X-rated, the chances of me resisting the urge to beg Leo to take me right here, bent over at the sink, will be slim to none. My hips squirm again, and Leo answers with another soft growl.

"Apologies," I murmur.

"I'm the one who should apologize," he says, rinsing the conditioner away.

"Why's that?"

"Because I lied to you." He shuts off the water, wrapping a towel around my damp hair before guiding me to stand in front of him. "I don't want to practice flirting."

"No?" I tell myself I'm dizzy because I was just bent over upside down, but that isn't the reason my head is spinning.

"No." Leo moves closer, pinning me between his powerful body and the cabinet behind me. "I don't want to practice. I just want to flirt with you. Even though I shouldn't."

"Why not?" I whisper, pulse racing in my throat.

"Because you're off-limits. You're human and fragile, and starting something with you would be a mistake."

"I'm not as fragile as you think," I say, pressing up on tiptoe to press a kiss to Leo's cheek, heart clutching as his breath rushes out with a soft, hungry sound.

He tilts his head, shifting his lips over mine, brushing them lightly back and forth in a teasing caress that makes my hormones stampede through my veins like a crash of charging rhinos.

"Eliza," he whispers, my name poetry on his lips. "God, I want—"

"Fucking starving!" The door to the second bedroom crashes open, sending Leo and I leaping apart as Rourke prowls into the kitchen, bound for the fridge. "Feel like I haven't eaten in years." He grunts as he pulls a bag of chilled blood from the top shelf and holds it up for inspection with a wrinkled nose. "And this? This is unacceptable for anything more than a day or two. I need to see my supplier about a few cases of the good bottled stuff, Leo. And Eliza needs a proper meal."

"You just want an excuse to cook," Leo says, plucking another towel from the counter beside me.

"Well, I *am* a great cook." Rourke's eyebrows bob up and down as his eyes flash in my direction. "So what do you say, Eliza? Up for a run to the store in a few? I want to choose the menu from whatever's fresh. Fresh is key."

"Leo is going to cut my hair, but I'm game after." I glance back to Leo. "How about you? Want to come along for the ride?"

"I'll stay here, mind the house, give the town gossips one less new face to wonder about." The hunger has vanished from his tone.

He seems to have recovered from our heated moment, but I'm still simmering. Sizzling. So starved for his touch that the fifteen minutes it takes for him to trim and shave my hair seems an eternity.

Every time his fingertips brush my ear, every time his breath warms my neck as he bends close, checking to make sure he's getting the line on the shaved portion of my head just right, my heart feels like it's going to swell right out of my rib cage.

By the time he's finally finished, my nerve endings are on fire, my nipples are tight, and my entire body is aching for more.

Instead, he sends me to the bathroom to check out his handiwork in the mirror alone. When I return to the kitchen to tell him I love it—it's edgy and fun and completely perfect—he's nowhere to be found.

Rourke is alone by the window, watching the last of the pink glow of dusk fade from the horizon.

"Where's Leo?" I try to play it cool, but even I can hear the hurt in my voice.

Rourke turns, a knowing smile curving his lips. "He went for a run on the beach, in an attempt to sweat out the urge to toss you on his bed and devour every sweet inch of you, I'm guessing."

My cheeks heat. "Oh, well…"

"But it won't work," Rourke says, swaying closer. "If it were just lust, maybe, but Leo doesn't work that way. If his dick's interested, his heart is already invested." He stops mere inches away, grinning down at me with a smile that's smug, irritating, and irresistible, all at the same time.

"And what about you, Mr. Rourke? How do your heart and dick behave?"

"Oh, they don't, love," he says in a wicked whisper that makes my pulse quicken as he pulls me close to murmur his next words against my temple. "They don't behave at all. But I don't think you want them to, do you?"

Wrapping my arms around his neck, I sigh, "No, I don't."

"Come on, then." He hugs me so tight my feet come off the floor. "I promise to misbehave all the way to the store and back. Make driving as difficult for you as possible."

I laugh as he sets me down. "Leerie wouldn't approve. She's a big fan of safe driving."

"And I'm a big fan of my hands all over your delicious body," Rourke says, chasing me, giggling, down the stairs to the garage.

True to his word, he makes driving difficult, almost as difficult as getting out of the car after we've been making out for a good twenty minutes in the parking lot of the Coop grocery. But no matter how hot the kissing gets, all our clothes stay on and "tasting" isn't mentioned again.

And somehow I know it won't be, not until Leo decides on his next move.

Now that Rourke knows his friend and future co-husband is interested in me, too, things have changed. Shifted. Become simultaneously more serious and infinitely more sexy. We're all thinking about it, no matter how vehemently we might deny it. We're all rolling the possibility over in our minds, imagining what it might be like to be together.

Together for more than a night or a week in a romantic lighthouse.

Together as three people bound for life.

It's crazy—I barely know them, at least in this way. We've always been just friends.

But as the days pass in a blur of self-defense training on the beach with Rourke, learning how to kick ass with Pearl with Leo, and playing so many board games with the pair of them that I start dreaming about Scrabble tiles and zooming around town in the tiny silver Monopoly car, it quickly becomes clear that "just friends" isn't a phrase that applies to us anymore.

Rourke's hand on my shoulder as he teaches me how to fight off an attacker who approaches from behind,

Leo's arms around me as he adjusts my grip on Pearl's handle, that moment in the early evening when we're all bumping against each other in the kitchen as they warm up a glass of O negative and I fix coffee before heading out to the deck to practice my ballet routine—all of it combines to leave me in a state of near constant arousal.

I drift around the lighthouse simmering, a pot about to boil over and make a mess on the stove.

It is a mess, this situation.

I can't stay a rhinoceros forever, and Leo and Rourke can't choose a normal woman, no matter how much they might want to. Our paths are destined to diverge, most likely sooner rather than later.

I know this, but it doesn't stop me from letting Rourke steal a kiss after he pins me to the sand for the hundredth time. It doesn't stop me from running naked into the ocean with Leo in celebration the day our "shifting practice" finally sees me slipping in and out of my rhino skin at will. The waves are freezing, but I'm so hot from Leo's gaze raking up and down my body I barely feel it.

I want him so much it hurts, but Leo only looks, flirts, and occasionally steals a relatively chaste kiss. He doesn't touch, let alone throw me on the bed and ravage me the way I fantasize about every morning as I struggle to fall asleep.

By the time we enter our second week of hiding, bringing me within spitting distance of the first day of the Miss U.S. Pageant, the sexual frustration is starting to drive me crazy.

I reach out to Leerie again—needing best-friend advice in a major way—but my texts continue to bounce, and I can't be sure my emails are getting through, either. According to Rourke, Fairy is behind the times when it comes to cell towers and internet connectivity. Leerie is out of pocket and so am I, trapped in this limbo world where real life seems like fantasy and impossible things feel more possible with every passing day.

If I don't get back to my normal life soon, I'm going to be in trouble.

Big trouble.

Double trouble...

oreplay used to be something my girlfriends and I complained about a lack of, sick of men who thought a few kisses and a quick pit stop at second base were enough to justify sliding into home.

Where was the romance? The sense of anticipation? The commitment to ensuring we were sufficiently excited that sex is *comfortable,* let alone pleasurable?

If you'd asked me back then, I would have insisted that I'd never be able to get enough foreplay.

Now, it's *killing* me.

Literally. It feels like I might die from frustrated longing.

It was bad enough last week, but the last few days things have gotten even worse, the tension ramping up until it feels like both Leo and Rourke have made it their mission in life to get me turned on and leave me idling, desperate for someone to press the gas pedal already.

At this point, I swear, I would sell my soul to be taken—hard and fast—up against a wall.

"Or sell a limb. At least a kidney," I mumble, unaware I've spoken aloud until Leo nudges my elbow and asks, "What's that?" raising his voice to be heard over the din at the bar. Ladies night at the Clam Shack is apparently quite the draw for the locals.

"Nothing." I force a smile as Leo draws me close, presumably to make more room for the man ordering a drink behind me. But at this point, I'm not entirely sure that he isn't just torturing me for the fun of it.

He and Rourke both.

No sooner has Leo gathered me to his chest than Rourke is suddenly behind me, hand resting on the curve of my hip, making my blood rush as he sets his empty glass on the bar. "Another round? Or are we ready to head home and start supper for Eliza?"

"Home," Leo says as I nod my agreement, already too dizzy with longing to waste energy on useless words.

"Good." Rourke holds up his now empty flask. "Because I'm out of secret extra-bloody bloody Mary mix. Almost out of the bottled stuff at home, too. If we stay much longer, I'll have to fetch another case from my supplier."

"I'm meeting with Jamal in the morning." Leo's arm loops around my waist, keeping me close as we sway toward the exit. "He thinks he's figured out who was behind the attempt on our lives, but he didn't want to risk that kind of conversation on the phone. You never know who's listening at the castle."

"The walls have ears," Rourke agrees, patting my

bottom before he reaches for the door leading out to the parking lot, sending another jolt of awareness surging through my already-frayed nerve endings. "Literally," he adds with a meaningful glance my way. "There's a room in the tower covered with ears nailed to the walls. Gloria used to keep them as trophies, back before whacking off pieces of your prisoners before sending them back to their people became socially unacceptable."

I shiver, even though the sea air outside is warm tonight. "She seemed so nice when I met her. It's hard to imagine her being so..."

"Ear thirsty?" Rourke grins, pinching my cheek when I stick out my tongue.

"Stop," I order, pulling away from Leo as we reach the car. "No more touching me."

"But you're so cute when your cheeks are flushed from too much whiskey," Rourke says, swaying closer. "And you smell so sweet with a little honey and peat in your blood."

"Fine, then no touching until we get home." I wrap my arms around his neck. He presses a kiss to my cheek while Leo circles around to the other side of the car, pretending not to notice.

"How much longer can this go on?" I hiss beneath my breath, pleading eyes boring into Rourke's.

"Until he decides to stop fighting himself and give in to the inevitable," Rourke whispers, squeezing my ass in his big hands. "But until then, the anticipation is fucking delicious, isn't it?"

"No, it isn't," I snap, refusing to smile when he slaps

my bottom and laughs that ridiculously infectious laugh of his.

"Just wait, love." Rourke winks as he releases me, reaching for the back door. "We'll be worth the wait. I promise you that."

But that's not what I'm worried about. I'm worried that something is going to happen to derail this seemingly inevitable collision, that I'm never going to know what it's like to be with one of these amazing men, let alone both of them.

That's what I want. Both of them.

Together.

At the same time.

I can't hide it from myself—or them—anymore. Promising myself to someone, anyone, even two people I care for as much as I care for Leo and Rourke, still scares the shit out of me, but I would very much like to roll around naked in bed with them for a few weeks and at least consider forever as an option.

Truth be told, I'm already considering it.

I could end their curse, and this isn't just lust for me. It never was. It's about these two people, my dear friends who, in just a little over a week, have made the lighthouse at the end of Sea Breeze Drive feel like home.

As I pull into the parking garage, my heartbeat slows and my heart fills with a rush of cozy warmth just like it did when I would swing through the cottage door after work and find Leerie at the stove making popcorn for a midnight movie.

"Pasta or stir fry?" Rourke asks as we ride the elevator up to the main floor.

"I can just heat up leftovers."

"Don't be ridiculous." Rourke's nose wrinkles, as if I've suggested opening a can of dog food for dinner.

"Seriously," I say with a laugh. "Leftovers are fine. I love leftovers. It's silly for you to go to all the trouble of cooking every night when I'm the only one eating."

"Shut up," Rourke says. "Seriously, shut that pretty mouth of yours before you make me angry. Pasta or stir fry? Answer now, or I'm going to choose for you."

"Pasta," Leo pipes up from my other side. "I like the way she smells after she's eaten garlic."

I turn to him, cheeks flushing. "Oh God, is it bad? The garlic stink? I had a friend in high school who reeked every time she ate anything with onions in it."

"I don't believe I said anything about a stink," Leo says as the elevator doors slide open. He takes my hand, threading his fingers through mine as he steps out into the small foyer. "I said I like it." He leans down, bringing his nose to linger above my neck as he inhales, setting off a hormone explosion, easily the fifth or sixth tonight. "It makes you smell like salt and earth and…"

"And?" I ask, my voice breathy.

"And other things." He pulls back, holding my gaze. My breath comes faster as he adds, "Things it's impolite to mention in public."

I'm about to remind him that we're not in public— we're in our home all alone except for Rourke, who is already bustling about in the kitchen, pulling ingredients from the fridge—when my phone screams at me from my purse.

Literally screams, like a beauty queen who just got an armpit wax.

I jump, and my eyes fly wide. "That's Eugene's ring," I say, frozen with a mixture of terror and hope.

"Then answer it," Leo says, gesturing urgently toward my purse.

"Right, right. Answering!" I rip open the zipper with trembling hands and fumble the phone from the side pocket, tapping the speaker button to make sure Leo and Rourke don't miss a second of this unexpected new development. "I'm here, Eugene. I really hope this is the call I've been waiting for."

"Hey, Eliza," he says, clearing his throat for a long, awkward moment that makes me want to reach through the screen and shake him. Couldn't he have taken care of his hemming and hawing before he dialed the phone? "Yeah, I think it's time."

"Time to turn me back into a normal person?" I ask, heart jerking as fear and hope wrestle near my lungs.

"Time to put your DNA back the way it was before, yes. I know the pageant stuff starts in a few days. Probably best if you're human for all of that."

I bite my lip, fighting the urge to squeal with happiness. Instead, I force the smile from my face and say in a remarkably calm voice, "Thank you. I appreciate that, Eugene. When would you like to meet?"

"Tomorrow at seven p.m. at my office at the university. We'll rock it out after I'm finished with advisor hours and before I have to be downtown for that modern art gala thing at eight."

My brows pull together as I shoot Leo a worried look. "Will that be enough time?"

"Oh yeah, totally," Eugene says. "We'll have time to

get you fully human and still grab a salad from the cafeteria after for dinner if you want."

I roll my eyes. As if I'm ever sharing a meal with that man again. But I'm all about keeping him happy until I'm back to normal so I say, "Um, yeah, maybe. Sure."

"Though, on second thought, you might not be hungry." He pauses before adding in a reluctant tone, "There will be some pain this time. No way to avoid it, really. The more you mess with the code, the more uncomfortable it gets."

Leo scowls at the phone as I ask, "How uncomfortable are we talking?"

"Minor burn uncomfortable," Eugene says, "maybe a little worse. But like I said, there's no avoiding it. Unless you want to stay a rhino-girl. Though, I honestly wouldn't recommend that. We don't know enough about the long-term effects of extreme DNA modification. There's not enough data for me to promise you won't wake up one morning with a rhino foot and never be able to change it back again, you know?"

"Right. And no, I don't want to stay a shifter." I shake my head, ignoring the sharp tug of regret at the back of my thoughts.

I can't stay a rhinoceros, not even for Leo and Rourke.

Yes, I've mostly learned to control the shifting now, but my rhino skin is never going to be a place I enjoy being. That body isn't something I chose. It was a punishment, forced on me by a man who wanted to hurt and humiliate me. And as much as I enjoy having a little extra weight to throw around when I need it, I don't want to be a supernatural creature or a superhero.

I just want to be Eliza, a human woman making her human dreams come true without having to worry about the long-term consequences of being a science experiment gone wrong.

So I promise to meet Eugene tomorrow and end the call.

I pull in a breath, intending to ask Leo what he thinks about Eugene's sudden change of heart, but when I look up, the foyer is empty. I move into the combination living room and kitchen, but there's no sign of him there, either.

"He went for a run," Rourke says softly. "And for once, I can't really blame him."

I nod, swallowing past the lump in my throat. I can't blame him, either, but running isn't going to help.

None of us can run from this. We just have to play the shitty cards Fate dealt us and hope the pain won't be too bad. That it will fade with time.

That it won't last the forever we aren't free to promise each other.

CHAPTER 18

*F*orty minutes later, I'm still pacing back and forth in front of the now-open windows, chewing on my thumb while Rourke moves easily around the kitchen, putting the finishing touches on enough food to feed ten people. Leo is back from his run and outside on the deck filling wine glasses—two with the red stuff vampires like and one with a ridiculously expensive Cabernet Rourke brought up from the wine cellar in celebration of Eugene's change of heart.

By tomorrow night I'll be human again.

I should be ecstatic.

Overjoyed.

Hooves over heels.

So why do I feel like I'm waiting for the other shoe to drop? And that the shoe isn't a shoe, but a giant steel beam suspended over my head, ready to crush me flat?

"This is good news," I mumble, reaching the corner by the stereo and turning to pace back toward the wet bar on the other end of the room. "Great news."

"Most excellent," Rourke says, cutting a cucumber into tiny slivers with swift rocks of his wrist.

"And Eugene sounded normal on the phone. Reasonable even," I continue. "So the chances that this is a trick to lure me to his office and do something terrible to me are pretty slim. And what can he do to me that he hasn't already done? And even if he were planning something sketchy, we're meeting after sundown so you and Leo can tag along. I'll be completely safe."

"As a babe in a cradle," Rourke agrees, squeezing lemon into the pan of simmering shrimp, sending a rush of garlic-scented goodness hissing into the air.

I flop into an armchair but almost immediately jump back to my feet, the down cushion too soft for my current state. "There is literally nothing that can go wrong. Right?" I cross to the island, bracing my arms on the marble countertop as I face Rourke across a sea of cutting boards.

"Something can always go wrong," he says pleasantly, "but we'll be on guard. And your ex is a coward. I seriously doubt he'll try anything while he knows he's being watched by three people who could kill him with their bare hands."

"Two," I correct, snagging a cucumber slice.

"Three." Rourke moves the shrimp pan to the other side of the stove and flips off the burner. "You're a natural in the ring, Eliza, even without Pearl. And you can control the shifting now. Worst case scenario, if for some reason Leo and I were out of the picture, you could shift and sit on the bastard."

"I don't want to sit on anyone. Not even Eugene," I

say before adding in a softer voice, "and I don't want you out of the picture."

"We wouldn't abandon you willingly."

"I know, I just..." I grab another cucumber, stress-nibbling the peel as I watch Rourke mix the shrimp into angel hair pasta.

"Just?" he prompts, dressing the salad with cucumber slices and then pushing the bowl toward me.

But I'm suddenly not hungry anymore.

I sag onto the stool beside me, chin propped in my hands. "I can't stay this way. Even though a part of me might want to."

"And we would never ask you to stay this way," Rourke says softly. "No matter how much we might want you to."

I search his face, feeling more torn apart with every passing second. I can't stay with them, but how am I ever going to leave? How am I going to walk out of here to meet Eugene tomorrow night knowing I'll never be coming back? Not to the lighthouse and not to this moment in time, when a future with two incredible men was close enough for me to taste it?

Once I'm human, that road will be closed to me forever. Barred and gated and secured with a lock so strong there will be no busting through it.

"Why don't you go take a bath," Rourke says after the tension has stretched on long enough to make me feel like my stomach is crawling up my throat. "Relax. I can heat the food up when you're ready."

"Okay," I whisper, sliding to the ground. With a last glance over my shoulder at Leo, who's watching the ocean below as if he expects the answer to our problems to emerge from the dark waves, I head for the bathroom.

But the warm water and massive bathtub offer no comfort tonight. I'm too on edge, too messed up, too filled with aching and longing and pain. It hurts, what's happening inside me. My heart feels like it's being torn apart by Kin Born wolves, ripped and shredded and left to bleed out on the cold ground.

Alone.

All alone.

Alone forever because who could ever compare to Leo and Rourke? What man—living or undead—could hold a candle to them? To my men?

But they aren't mine, and they never will be.

I'm crying so hard I don't realize what's happening until it's too late. One moment, I'm a grieving girl in a half-filled bathtub. The next, I'm half a rhinoceros, shattering the antique tub, water gushing over the tile as I fill the bathroom to maximum capacity.

CHAPTER 19

I've barely had time to turn off the water and begin to take in the damage when a fist pounds on the door and Rourke shouts, "Eliza! Are you all right? What happened?"

"Bad things," I call back, voice breaking on a sob. "Very bad."

"Open the door."

"I can't," I whimper. "It's locked and I can't reach the handle."

"Stand back," he says, hitting the door hard enough to rattle it on its hinges. "I'm coming in."

"No, don't!" I wail, floundering on the ground—a rhino from the waist down and a woman from the waist up. If Rourke sees me like this, like the world's most hideous mermaid or satyr or whatever you'd call a rhino-girl hybrid, I'll die of shame.

Even though I didn't do this to myself. Even though I can't help it. Even though I know he won't judge me or hate me or laugh at me.

The door splinters open with a creak and a crunch, spilling Rourke through the opening. He freezes just inside, taking in the destruction for a beat before throwing back his head and laughing so hard it makes my back leg start to twitch, which knocks over the toilet, which makes him laugh even harder, which makes the tears pressing at the backs of my eyes spill over.

"Don't laugh," I say, sniffling into the bath mat. "It's not funny."

"Oh, but it is, love." He crouches beside me, gently brushing the hair from my face. "I didn't think anything could make me laugh tonight, but I should have known better." He cups my cheek in his hand. "You always make me laugh."

"I ruined your bathroom," I say with a sniff.

"I don't care." He pats my flank, where the rhino skin is so thick I usually wouldn't be able to feel a gentle touch. But I do feel it, and when I look down, I see my animal body gliding back into its fully human form, leaving me naked and shivering on the soaked bathroom floor.

But Rourke doesn't seem to mind.

"Your clothes are getting all wet," I whisper as he pulls me into his lap.

"I don't care about that, either," he says, his hands skimming up and down my sides. "And I don't care about the curse or the future or doing what other people tell me to do. Not right now. I only care that this may be my last chance to show you what you do to me. What you mean to me."

He cups my breast. I shudder as the force of all my

denied longing rises inside of me like a giant wave, threatening to destroy everything in its path.

"What about Leo?' I ask as I thread fingers into his hair.

"I'm my own man," he says, rising to his feet with me in his arms. "And I'm tired of waiting for permission to make love to you from anyone but you."

I cling to his shoulders as he turns, carrying me out of the bathroom through the broken door, unable to believe this is really happening. That I'm really going to have Rourke in my bed, his hands all over me, his body moving against mine.

"So do I have it?" he asks, stopping at the end of the bed.

"Have what?' I ask, trembling as he hugs me closer.

"Your permission, love," he says, his voice rough. "Your permission to make you come so hard for me you'll never forget this night. Not if you live for another hundred years."

I cup Rourke's face in my hands, dragging his lips down to mine, kissing him with a passion I hope assures him that my answer is "hell, yes."

CHAPTER 20

*L*ips fused, tongues dancing hard and deep, Rourke and I tumble onto the giant bed. The cool sheets caress my bare skin as my fingers thread through the silk of his shaggy hair, sending fresh waves of arousal dumping into my blood. His hands skim over my body, setting fires in their wake—on my swollen breasts, my tight nipples, the swell of my hip, the curve of my ass.

He curses, his grip tightening on my backside. "You're so fucking beautiful. I want my hands, my mouth, all over you."

"Yes, please," I whisper against his lips, my breath catching as he cups my breast, his thumb teasing over my electric tip. "Touch me everywhere."

"Everywhere?" His other hand teases lower, over the mound of my bottom and up again, getting close to where I ache, but not nearly close enough.

"Please," I beg, raking my nails down his muscled back. "Touch me."

"Touch you where, love?"

I shudder, the pulse between my legs twisting into a knot I know only he can untangle. "Touch me there."

"Here?" He squeezes my breast again, dropping his head to flick his tongue over my nipple.

I moan, thoughts quickly becoming as tangled as the rest of me as he does it again, and then again. I writhe beneath him, my hips squirming restlessly as my thighs grow slicker, hotter. "God, yes."

"Not God, love, but by the time I'm done, you'll be remembering me in your prayers," Rourke says, a hint of his Irish accent sneaking into the words. Into the lilt of his voice. Into the way his fingers finally dance across those last few inches of oh-so-intimate territory to press inside me.

And, of course, fingers can't literally have an accent, but it feels like they do. His touch is foreign, different than anything I've experienced before, but in the best way. His fingers are lyrical, magical, and as he glides deeper—cursing again in soft appreciation, as if he's never felt anything as lovely as how wet I am for him— my heart breaks open and my secrets come sighing out into the air.

"I've wanted this since the beginning," I confess, melting into a puddle of bliss at the sweet friction.

"Me, too. From the second you walked into your kitchen on that first night, I couldn't keep my eyes off of you. I was supposed to be courting your best friend, ending a curse and securing the future of my people, but all I could think about was your laugh, your smile, the way you blush when you tell a dirty joke." He nips my neck, my clavicle. "You in your swimsuit by the lake in the moonlight, in that wee skirt you wore roller skating, in those cut-off shorts the night you made banana bread, bending over to pull your muffins out of the oven with a flour handprint on your ass." He shudders against me. "God, the muffin day... It almost killed me."

I giggle. "Food prep fetish?"

"*You* fetish," he murmurs, making my heart skip a beat. "You drive me crazy, Eliza. I want to be inside you so badly it's tearing me apart."

I gasp, clinging to his shoulders as he fucks me harder with his hand, my hunger roaring loud enough to make my bones tremble. "Me, too," I breathe into his neck. "I've never wanted anyone, anything like this." I'm so worked up I could come right now if I let myself.

But I don't want to. I want to draw out this moment of almost-there, almost-together, almost-us.

Us.

Damn it, why can't we be us? Ten days away from the world with Leo and Rourke have shown me how good we could be together. How normal and how extraordinary, all at the same time. Whether we're sorting tiles for a game of Scrabble or doing laundry or working to blend self-defense with a touch of magic, every moment with them is special. Perfect. Home.

For the first time in my life, I feel like I'm exactly where I'm supposed to be.

So maybe I'm not the person I thought I'd be when I found forever. So what? There are worse things than being a shifter with an occasionally unpredictable, highly destructive rhino form. There is living the rest of my life without feeling the way I feel when I'm with Rourke and Leo.

Rourke's thumb glides over my clit and I see stars and comets and other astrological phenomena streaming across the ceiling.

I want to ask him if he feels the way I feel—like we can make it work, no matter how wild things might get if my DNA goes wonky someday—but the words won't come because he won't stop touching me.

Taking me.

Transporting me to a world where there are no questions, only answers, and every one is his name.

"I...I can't..." My head falls back, and my breath rushes out. "I can't think. When you... I can't... Oh God..."

"Then don't think, love," he whispers against my jaw as his wicked, wonderful fingers write poetry between my legs, proving all that other loveliness was just the opening act. *"Feel.* Feel what I do to you, darling girl. Fuck, you're so wet. I can't wait to feel you come for me."

I cry out, back arching off the bed as I lift into his hand, my release so intense the stars burn brighter and the planets align, and for a brief, shining moment, everything makes perfect sense. I step outside of the chaos and drama and danger that's plagued the past few weeks, and I see the truth.

I see two men who care about me. Two men who I'm already mad about, who can give me everything I need and then some. And, as long as I have the guts to stay a one-of-a-kind shifter, I can help them reclaim everything they've lost.

I can give their people a future, and we can give each

other an eternity of love unlike anything I've ever imagined.

All I have to do is give up my human life.

Anxiety dumps into my bloodstream, mixing with the pleasure still humming there, and I feel so torn that when Rourke cups my face in his warm hand and asks, "What's wrong, love?" I can't speak right away.

But no one ever said love was going to be easy. And I'm not about to let fear steal the magic from this moment.

"Nothing's wrong." Pushing the confusion away, I reach between us, finding the hot, hard length of him and stroking him up and down.

His eyelids flutter in response, but he still shakes his head. "We can stop. Things don't have to go any further tonight. I can wait until you're ready."

"I'm ready," I whisper.

"Are you sure?" Rourke asks, his eyes glittering a warning. "Because if I take you, I'm going to taste you, love. I won't be able to stop myself." His jaw clenches. "You smell too sweet. Like summertime. Like sin. I swear, I want you flowing down my throat almost as much as I want to feel you coming on my cock."

"I want that, too. So much." I stroke him harder, a heady rush of power coursing through me when he groans and a slick bead of pre-cum appears at the tip of him. I swirl it around his plump head as I reach down, cupping his balls with my other hand and squeezing lightly. "I'm ready. Please, Rourke. I'm so ready for you."

He growls, a low, hungry growl that makes my pulse spike and things low in my body wind into knots all over again.

And then Rourke is pinning my hands to the mattress and kneeing my thighs apart. And then his cock—so hot and hard and thick—is nudging at where I'm swollen, aching, dying for him. And then he's inside me, *finally* inside me, stretching my inner walls until the most delicious fullness spreads throughout my entire being and the last of my defenses come tumbling down.

Being naked with a man has never felt so right, so incredible and perfect.

"Yes, oh yes," I cry out to the rafters, wrapping my legs around his waist and pulling him closer at the end of every thrust, already knowing I'm never going to get him close enough.

I want him under my skin, as close and dear as every beat of my heart.

"Eliza. Sweet, beautiful Eliza," he murmurs against my neck with a kiss that burns silky sweet.

But it isn't just a kiss, I realize as bliss floods me. My nipples bead tighter and my eyes feel like they're going to sparkle right out of my head. I've heard the gossip about vampire boyfriends, and how "once he bites, you don't go back," but I had no idea it would be like this.

Like I've grown a second set of nerve endings, even more sensitive than the first. Like I'm surfing a mile-high pleasure wave, wild and fearless and free. Like I'm coming where he's kissing me at the same time as my body locks down around his thickness, my release so intense I scream his name loud enough to wake the dead.

More than loud enough to alert the very awake and very sensitive undead ears out on the deck...

I don't mean to taunt Leo with what's going on in

here without him. I simply can't control my mouth or stop the flood of "Yes, Rourke, God Rourke, more Rourke," rushing out of my mouth.

But actions have consequences, even actions you haven't thought through completely—like fucking one of your vampire almost-boyfriends while your other vampire almost-boyfriend is just two rooms away.

I know about unintended consequences better than anyone. It's how I ended up a kiddie pageant queen when I'd rather have been hiding in my room reading fairy tales and sewing princess costumes. And how I ended up a rhinoceros after dating one douchebag too many.

So when my eyes finally dazzle open post-orgasm to see Leo standing at the foot of the bed, his eyes blazing and his bare chest as flawless and beautiful as sculpted marble in the light filtering in from the bathroom, I'm not surprised.

Or scared. Or worried. Or inclined to second-guess myself.

Because this? Rourke crying out as he comes inside me while Leo's eyes penetrate my soul in ten different ways? This is the best thing that has ever happened to me.

At least, the best thing to happen to me yet...

The thought fizzes through me like the first sweet, seductive sip of champagne on a hot summer night, and I lift my arm, holding out a hand to Leo, reaching for what I want.

What I need, more than I've ever needed anything in this whole, big, wide world.

CHAPTER 21

For a split second, I don't think Leo is going to come to me. To us.

His gaze falls to the floor, he takes a step back, and in my mind's eye, I see him turning to walk away, taking the crushed pieces of my heart with him.

But he doesn't turn. He doesn't run.

He reaches for the close of his pants, popping the button and slowly drawing down the zipper.

And then he pushes his pants to the floor, and I get a good look at the size of the bulge pressing against the seam of his boxer briefs, and my belly fills with wildly beating wings.

Rourke isn't small by any means, but Leo is massive, so thick and long that the sight of what he's packing would usually be anxiety-provoking. But this isn't a normal night or a normal man, and imagining all that pulsing need gliding inside me only makes me ache.

"About time, Poplov," Rourke purrs. "I could use a

few minutes to pull myself together before I make our girl come for me again."

Our girl...

I've dreamt of being called someone's girl in that affectionate, possessive, can't-get-enough-of-this-woman tone my entire life. Instead, I got losers and users and a mad scientist with a sadistic streak. I was starting to believe I'd never find one man who thought I was something special, let alone two.

But as Leo crawls onto the bed beside us, hunger and uncertainty mixing in his eyes, I know he feels it—the rightness, the sweetness, the happiness just waiting for us to reach out and grab it.

"And maybe it doesn't have to be perfect to be good?" I murmur, as Rourke gently pulls out of me, rolling to my other side with tender kisses on my shoulder, my forehead, the top of my wild hair. I gaze up into Leo's incomparable eyes as he lengthens himself beside me on the mattress, propped up on one arm. "Maybe it's okay that the thing that makes me special is also destructive and hard to handle and occasionally gross?"

Leo brushes the hair gently from my face before gliding his fingertips from my temple to my chin, and I'm breathless at that one simple, innocent touch. "You're never gross. You're beautiful," he says, bringing tears stinging back into my eyes.

"I want to save the rhinos as much as anyone, but not even I think they're beautiful." I blink faster, words getting harder to hold onto as Leo's hand moves lower, skimming down my throat to trace the line of my clavicle back and forth. "Noble. Powerful. And um, I..." My pulse races and my breasts go full and heavy as Leo's fingers head south, whispering into the valley between them. "But not beautiful."

"They are to me." He holds my gaze as his hand comes to cup my breast oh-so-gently, making my heartbeat stutter. "*You* are to me. I see you, Eliza."

"I see you, too," I say, lifting my hands to his dear face. "And I know you've been through hell and you're terrified of going there again, but..." I swallow, praying that the words come out right. "I can't promise not to die, but I can promise to be careful and to listen to you and to do everything I can to stay safe. But more importantly, I can promise to care about you and be there for you and make however much time we have together something special."

"Because that's what makes life worth living," Rourke says gently from behind me, his hand curving over my hip. "Something special. Some*one* special."

"Is this what you want? You're sure?" Leo asks, his thumb circling my nipple.

"She's what I want," Rourke says. "The only one I want."

"Not you, asshole," he says, his gaze still fixed on my face. "Eliza, is this what you want? Two men who will never see you in the sunlight? Who will never have a life that's easy or simple or safe? Who will never give you children or grow old with you or even promise to die and leave you in peace someday?"

Lips quivering, Leo's handsome face blurring with tears, I whisper, "I don't want to be left in peace. I don't want simple or safe. I just want you. Both of you."

"Then you shall have us," Leo says, his lips meeting mine for a long, slow, deep and delicious kiss that is more than skin on skin. It's a promise, a vow that no matter where the road leads from here, we'll walk down it together.

It's so beautiful, so real and right that twin trails of wetness stream down my cheeks as Leo pulls away, gazing down at me with a mixture of love and desire.

"Thank God." Rourke presses a kiss to my neck, summoning a soft sob from my throat with my next breath. "Don't cry, sweetheart," he adds in a thick whisper. "I'm going to make it my mission in life to make sure you never cry again, not another day in your life."

"But beautiful things always make me cry." I glance over my shoulder to meet Rourke's gaze. "And you two are the most beautiful things I've ever seen. I love you." I glance back to Leo. "Both of you."

"And we love you." Leo's hand skims down my belly. "And I'm going to show you how much. Spread your legs, Eliza, let me touch you."

And he does. Oh God, he does.

And then he kisses me—*there*—and I'm done. Lost. Found.

Home.

I'm seconds from coming a third time when I reach for Leo, tugging at his soft hair. He slides up to me, lips devouring mine as he rolls onto his back, drawing me on top of him, moaning as I spread my legs, setting my slick pussy on a collision course with the thick, hot ridge of his cock.

"I want you so much." I rock against his erection, belly swooping as his thickness twitches against me, and Leo groans, his fingers digging deep into my hips.

"Then take me, beautiful," he says, his voice husky

as he lifts me and guides me back down. The head of his cock glides through where I'm so slick, so wet, and then he's pushing inside, filling me completely. My heart sings and the room spins.

And as we rock together, eyes locked, my hands braced on his chest, I have never felt more beautiful or powerful or worthy. I'm where I belong, naked and unashamed with two amazing men I once thought would be forever out of my league.

But I underestimated them, and myself.

I may not be as beautiful and clever as Leerie or as powerful or magical as the other women on a shortlist of one-in-a-million girls, but my heart is as big as they come. Big enough to bring back Leo's smile and to banish the shadows from Rourke's dancing eyes. Strong enough to stand beside them no matter how many people try to tear us apart.

I know right then that I won't be meeting Eugene tomorrow night, at least not to have him change me back. I'm going to stay a shifter, stay weird and wonderful and happy with my two precious loves.

I cry out as I come seconds before Leo, the feel of his cock jerking inside me drawing out the pleasure for what feels like ages.

And then, before I've fully come back into my buzzing skin, I find myself cradled against Rourke in a spoon position as he pushes into me from behind, and Leo is kissing my breasts, and soon I lose track of whose hands are where.

I'm lost in a sea of happiness and bliss, adrift with my favorite two people, determined never to set foot on shore again.

CHAPTER 22

*H*ours later—many hours and many orgasms —I tiptoe out onto the deck in the dark, pulling Leo's robe tighter around me against the chill, and then pulling it even closer because it smells like him.

I'm sure I've been this happy before at least once or twice in my life, but I can't remember it.

The cynical voice in my head insists I'm just high on endorphins and sex chemicals and I'll be back to normal again come morning, but I know that isn't true. I'm high on love and hope and the thrilling, adventure-packed future stretching out in front of me.

And yes, I'm still scared, too, but fear is a part of every great adventure. If it weren't, adventure would be called "running errands" or "the same stuff I did yester-day." And yes, a part of me wonders if Leo and Rourke would still want me if I were just Eliza, an ordinary girl incapable of breaking the curse on their shivers, but that's the kind of wondering that needlessly, pointlessly wrecks happiness.

That's like fretting whether Leo and Rourke would still love me if I were tall and slim instead of short and curvy, or if I were a non-driving person like Leerie instead of a speed demon who has never met a stop sign I won't run if no one is coming from the other direction.

I am who I am, all parts considered, and that's who my men want. Me.

I've never felt luckier. Safer. Or more at home in my own skin.

I lean against the deck railing, watching the moon dazzle across the tops of the waves, doing my best to commit every moment of this night to memory. I don't want to forget a second, a heartbeat. I close my eyes, replaying every kiss, every touch, every time I looked into Leo or Rourke's eyes and saw clear evidence that I wasn't alone in these feelings, this love.

To say I'm distracted would be an understatement, but I still have rhino-enhanced hearing. I should have heard them.

But I didn't.

One second I'm relaxed and rocking a hard orgasm buzz, the next there's a sharp prick in my arm and a flood of heat in my veins. I spin, ready to scream, but a hand is already slamming down over my mouth.

Eugene's hand.

I growl his name, glaring at him as I sag in his arms. Whatever evil was in that needle is working fast.

"I've got it, let's go." Jamal's face comes into view behind Eugene's, a dark moon blotting out the field of stars. I see that he's clutching Pearl in one ringed hand and wonder what's happened to Leo and Rourke.

"Hurry," Jamal adds in a whisper as the stars begin to spin. "Before they wake up."

Before they wake up...

Leo and Rourke are safe. Asleep, for now, but they'll come for me. Save me. Get me away from these two cowardly ass-wipes before they can do whatever awful thing they came to do to me.

"You left the letter?" Eugene scoops me up into his arms, starting toward the stairs leading down to the beach.

"Of course I left it," Jamal snaps. "I don't forget things, doc. They'll wake up to a letter from Blondie saying she's running away to start a normal life, and we'll all be back on track to getting what we want with no one dying in the process."

The not dying part sounds good, but the rest of it is awful.

So awful, that if I could keep my eyes open, I'd be crying.

But I can't.

Keep...

Them open...

The poison rushing through my veins reaches up and snatches my lids closed. I wink out a beat later, succumbing to the drugs that wrap my brain up in a soft, dark, oh-so-scary hug.

CHAPTER 23

I wake up fast, already sputtering and thrashing, even before my thoughts catch up with my body and I remember the hands in the dark.

The needle in my vein.

The sound of the ocean crashing as I was carried away from Leo and Rourke. Away from home.

I squirm, straining to lift my arms from my sides, but struggling is useless. I'm bound to a heavy chair with thick rope wrapped around my torso and what feels like Pearl snuggled into the hollow of my back between my spine and the chair's wooden back. I summon a swirl of pre-shift energy into my bones, and an answering golden glow blares to life behind me.

Pearl is here, all right, and she's being used to trap me, to keep me from busting into rhino form—or busting out of here before my captors return.

A quick glance around, craning my neck as much as I'm able while wrapped up tight, reveals bare concrete floors in both directions, with nothing else to look at aside from a large picture window that stretches from one side of the wide room to the other. There's no sign of a door, even, but there must be one somewhere in the shadows that hulk close behind me, breathing down my neck, making me grateful for the few faint stars still twinkling in the sky outside, for any spark of light in the darkness.

I can't remember ever being this scared, even when I was being chased by the Kin Born or when they invaded the castle grounds. At least then I could move, fight, run. Now I'm trapped, tied up and helpless to defend myself only a few hours after promising Leo that I would do everything in my power to stay safe.

Leo...

Will he and Rourke believe the note Jamal left behind?

Or will they know that it's a fake and that I'm in trouble?

Will it matter, either way, considering sunrise is starting to smudge the horizon outside with a faint brownish-orange?

The very familiar horizon...

Blinking the cobwebs from my aching head, I scan the skyline, struggling to remember where I've seen this view before and where I might be in the city. There's the Seattle needle, the jagged teeth of the skyscrapers downtown, the ridge of the marine barriers holding back the rising sea...

Before I can sort it out, the lights in the room flicker on with a series of sharp hums, and I hear a heavy door open and slam closed behind me. I squint in the sudden light, wincing as I catch a glimpse of my reflection, now visible in the glass in front of me. I look rough—my face swollen and red, my eyes puffy, and my hair a rat's nest of such epic proportions it blocks out the features of the people behind me until they're so close I can smell them.

I catch Eugene's coffee-and-too-much-deodorant scent first, followed by a delicate lavender-rose that sends a chill through my bones.

My nose knows that combo, even if my brain is a few steps behind, so I'm not completely surprised when the Strife shiver's master circles around my chair, her head of tight, gray-gold curls covered by a floral kerchief.

With her raincoat, yellow galoshes, and matching yellow-framed glasses, Gloria looks adorable, a touch matronly, even. But of course, she is neither.

She is evil. Pure, lying, back-stabbing evil.

"You're the one who let the Kin Born onto the castle grounds," I say, my voice scratchy.

"I did. Apologies, sweetheart," she says, not looking apologetic at all, "but it couldn't be helped. A master has to do what a master has to do."

"A master should protect her people," I shoot back. "You tried to kill Leo and Rourke."

"And you, darling." Jamal sashays into view behind the master, his arms crossed and his lips pursed. "Those big bad wolves could have gotten around to chomping on you if I hadn't stepped in to the save the day. If I were you, I'd start looking out for number one, not those boys who couldn't care less about you."

"Shut up," I snap, my head throbbing too fiercely to whip up a more eloquent comeback. "You're worse than Sven. At least he never pretended to be my friend."

"Oh, but I am your friend. I'm the one who's got your best interests at heart," Jamal says as he makes a come-hither motion to someone behind me. "Get over here, doc."

A moment later, Eugene skulks into view, looking even more exhausted than I feel. But then, he's the only garden-variety human involved in this kidnapping. The rest of us have supernatural power to pull from.

If only I could pull on mine enough to shift and crush every one of these jerks under my rhino feet.

I wiggle my shoulders, hoping for a miracle, but Pearl is lodged tight.

"Explain yourself to your girl, Eugene," Jamal says, nodding my way. "But make it quick. The sun waits for no man, and certainly no vampire."

"Master Gloria is the one who asked me to turn you," he says, shifting uncomfortably from one foot to the other, his gaze fixed on the floor.

I rear back as far as I'm able, my head pressing against the chair. "What?"

"She knew Leo and Rourke were interested in you," he says with a limp shrug. "She came to me, offering to fund my infusion research if I made you a one-of-a-kind shifter, one who could help the princes break the curse. So..."

"So you *sold* me?" I ask, incredulous. It hurt badly enough when I thought Eugene had betrayed me because he wanted me back. To know he did it for money somehow makes it so much worse. "So those texts about wanting a second chance were all bullshit?"

"I'm sorry." He glances up, what looks like real regret in his brown eyes. "I was angry with you for breaking up with me. And for the way you looked at them. Leo and Rourke. You never looked at me like that, Piglet. And they were supposed to be Leerie's boyfriends. It wasn't right."

"You don't get to preach to me about right and wrong." I'm about to launch into a laundry list of all the ways he's proven to be morally bankrupt, when Gloria cuts in.

"But right or wrong, our plan failed. That became clear as soon as you stopped by the club that night. I called Leo later, jazzed to talk new possibilities, but he refused to even consider a courtship with you." She shakes her head, lip curling closer to her upturned nose. "I'd given him a woman he clearly wanted, but as soon as she was a viable option—" She holds up a fist, her fingers popping open in an exploding motion. "Poof! Suddenly, Mr. Impossible to Please wasn't tempted anymore. Suddenly you were 'off-limits' and needed to be protected—using shiver resources—while he found a way to reverse your transformation."

Gloria sighs, her arm falling to her side. "I knew then that it wasn't the selection of women that was the problem. It was a prince who refused to make a fucking effort or put his people first. So...I made the call to eliminate Leo. And Rourke. He's been part of the problem, too—refusing to push Leo or move to secure an alliance without his approval."

"It's a marriage, Gloria," I say, a humorless laugh bursting from my chest, "not a membership in the fruit of the month club. You can't push someone into love without their approval."

"Love is a luxury our shivers can't afford." The

master rolls her shoulders back. "We don't make new vampires with love, doll face, we make them with a supernatural birthright that was stolen from us by a bitch of a witch. It's past time for us to take back our power. As the guardian of hundreds of lives, I made a decision to give our people a real chance at survival with someone else as my second-in-command."

"And then you ran away with our boys," Jamal said with a sigh. "And played house with them and fell in love with them, and for a while, we thought things might work out, after all. Even me." He motions to his forehead with two fingers. "Judging from everything I'd seen of the future, it looked like you three would tie the knot and the curse would be broken. And then Eugene showed up on our doorstep."

"The new code isn't stable, Eliza," Eugene explains, again with seemingly sincere regret. "All of my test subjects, every single one, is suffering reversion symptoms."

Jamal circles his hand, motioning him to keep going. "And? Tell her the rest, sunshine."

"And some of them are...dying," Eugene says, his contrition suddenly making more sense. "But not if I step in to rewrite the genetic code myself, first," he adds in a rush. "If I put your DNA back the way it was before you start glitching too hard, you'll be fine. It's only if we let the code degrade on its own that it becomes a problem."

"Yeah, I'd call dying a problem," I say, my pulse twitching in my throat.

"That's why I arranged the meet-up tomorrow." Eugene's focus slides Jamal's way. "But then Jamal called and said we should move it up. That we might already be on borrowed time."

"The partial shift in the bathtub," Jamal explains. "It's one of the first signs of a collapse in your code."

My cheeks heat and my skin crawls beneath Leo's soft robe. "You saw..." I shake my head, swallowing hard. "You were watching me? Us? The whole time?"

"I wanted to give Leo and Rourke a second chance," Gloria says, crossing to stand in front of me, her jaunty galoshes squeaking. "They seemed to care for you and you for them. I was willing to give it a little time, see if a connection would develop. And it did..." She sighs as she leans down, bringing her face even with mine, her eyes filled with a resigned sadness. "And then this shit had to happen. I'm sorry, Eliza. I was happy for you, kid, but you can't survive as a shifter, and as a human woman you're of no use to me."

"So what now?" Terror and misery electrify my nerves. "You kill me?"

She smiles, a hard, no-nonsense smile that makes my heart skip a beat. "No, doll. I'm not that ruthless. No matter what you've heard." She stands, nodding toward Eugene. "First, the doc will fix your genetic code. Then Jamal will see you settled in another city under another name. You'll have a home, a monthly income, everything you need, so long as you don't attempt to contact Leo or Rourke. It'll be easier for them to move on if they think you left of your own free will."

"They won't believe it," I say, tears pressing at the backs of my eyes. "They'll look for me. They won't let me go that easily, not without at least saying goodbye."

I know I'm being crazy—arguing the case for Gloria to kill me—but I can't help it. I don't want the life she's offering, a life without love. I've only just found Leo and Rourke, just barely begun to discover what this kind of happiness feels like. The thought of living the rest of my life without it feels like a knife carving my heart, still beating, from my chest.

"Maybe," Gloria says, her gaze going cold. "But I've already found that death makes Leo less likely to move on. So we'll just have to see what a Dear John letter will do."

The meaning of her words hits, and my internal organs shrivel inside me like grapes left too long in the cruel heat of the sun. "How could you? How could you do that to him? To her? They were innocent. In love. They were going to start a family."

"And Leo was next in line to rule after Prince Thomas got caught out in the sun," Gloria says, unflinching. "And he refused to consider keeping Eleanor as a mistress while he found a new mate with the Famine shiver's prince. It was either kill her, and get him on track to fulfilling his destiny, or kill him and lose another member of my rapidly dwindling shiver. So I did what I thought best. He gave me no choice."

"There's always a choice." Tears fill my eyes. "You're so powerful and clearly no dummy. You could have figured out another way to get what you wanted besides murdering a woman and leaving her husband shattered for the rest of his life."

"Not for the rest of his life," Gloria says, satisfaction firming up her features. "Leo learned to love you. He'll learn to love another after you're gone. I've already found someone who might do, another curvy blonde to make him forget the one who broke his heart and ran away." She steps back with a tip of her head. "But this one was born incomparable. We can't afford to waste any more time on lab rat mistakes." She lifts a hand to Eugene, holding up two fingers. "You have two hours before her flight leaves. Jamal will supervise. If you'd like your bonus, and for your ex-girlfriend to remain among the living, I suggest you get to work."

Without another word, or another glance spared for me, Gloria turns to leave, galoshes squeaking.

"They'll see you for what you are," I call after her, vision blurring as tears spill down my cheeks. "Leo and Rourke will see the truth, and they'll make you pay for what you've done."

Gloria pauses but doesn't look back as she speaks. "Could be right. But by then you will be a distant memory, Eliza. Or a dead girl. The choice is yours. I hope you choose wisely. I'd hate to snuff out your light, crackerjack, but I will. In a heartbeat."

I lift my chin, jaw clenched, trying to look tough. But I'm not tough, and tears still trail softly down my face. Obviously, I'm not a threat to anyone. I'm just a normal girl whose brief moment of being big and strong enough to take on the bad guys is almost over.

Gloria knows it, and I know it, and no amount of stiff-upper-lipping will stop what's about to happen. So I cry.

Why not? There's no shame in having feelings. There's shame in kidnapping people and tying them up and taking away their choices, but not in a few tears and a bucketful of regret. Still, I can't help thinking—if only

I'd trained harder, fought harder, loved harder while I had the chance.

If I had, I might still be with Leo and Rourke.

But now, I'll never see them again. I will live the rest of my life in hiding from the men I love or die trying to contact them. It's no choice. No life. It would be more merciful to kill me now and put me out of my misery.

And I suspect Gloria knows that, too.

Without another word, she turns and walks away, squeaking across the floor and out through the door I can't see.

And then Jamal is standing beside me, gently brushing the tangles from my hair before winding it into a bun on my head, reminding me of when Leo cut my hair, and the tears fall even faster. "It's okay, girl. You're going to be fine. Men are more trouble than they're worth, anyway, especially vampires. I'm telling you, you're dodging a bullet, no matter how much it hurts right now."

I don't respond, biting the inside of my cheek as Eugene swabs my wrist with alcohol, apologizing again and again as he hooks me up to an IV drip that will put me back the way I was before. Soon I will be just an ordinary girl, a not-at-all-incomparable person. I won't be ending any curses. I won't be changing history or the course of two men's lives.

And eventually, they will forget me. Maybe not today or tomorrow, but in a year or two, a decade at most, Leo and Rourke will have moved on so thoroughly that they'll be able to hear the name "Eliza" and not think of me. I'll just be someone they spent a hot night with by the sea, the woman they thought they could love until she wrote them a double-Dear-John letter and ran away.

As the medicine burns through my veins, unscrambling my cells, I cry out, but it's not the physical pain that makes my voice raw and ragged.

It's my heart. My breaking, shattering, splintering heart.

The heart that is so filled with despair that, at first, it doesn't know how to respond when two dark shadows holding matching baseball bats stride into view across the parking lot outside, silhouetted against the murky-gold of impending dawn.

Shadows with Rourke's wild hair and Leo's broad shoulders...

CHAPTER 24

*M*y pulse stutters, and the air rushes from my lungs with a suddenness that leaves me breathless.

I've been body slammed by hope, and before I can remember how to inhale, Leo and Rourke are leaping up to the windows, swinging their weapons around to strike the glass with supernatural force. There's a flash of light and a sonic boom, and then the window collapses in slow motion, shards cascading to the floor where they skitter and surge, swirling around the ankles of the men standing slack-jawed on either side of my chair.

Eugene cringes, arms flying up to cover his face long after it's too late to do any good. A hot second later, he drops the blood pressure monitor in his hand and bolts.

"Wait! Unhook me!" I shout after him, craning my head over my shoulder. "Eugene! Pull the needle out before you run away, you asshole!"

But Eugene's footsteps continue to fade to thuds in the distance, proving he's as gutless and awful as ever.

Unfortunately, Jamal isn't as easily frightened away.

I turn back to the battle breaking out in front of me, fighting to focus as the burning sensation in my veins gets hotter, sharper, feeling like a thousand tiny fire-breathing dragons have been set loose beneath my skin. Jamal is coming out blazing, shooting fire from his third eye, but Leo and Rourke are dodging and deflecting with two seriously badass aluminum bats.

But of course, they aren't normal bats, a fact made clear as Leo knocks a thunderbolt of flame back Jamal's way with a *thwack* that would make any major league player proud.

"They brought your big brothers, Pearl." I blink against the sweat running down my forehead to drip into my eyes. "We're going to be free in no time."

I suck in a shallow breath and let it out as slowly as I can, fighting to calm my racing pulse, but I'm no Zen master. My mind isn't strong enough to stop the madness surging through my body, unraveling me at the cellular level.

As Leo and Rourke fight for their lives—and mine—I clench my jaw and struggle to hold back the scream clawing its way up my throat, but it's a battle I can't win. The pain is wild, unrelenting, reason-eclipsing. I cling to my sanity long enough to fear that this agonizing pain is a sign that things are going hideously awry in my genome, and then I become the scream.

I'm pure pain and rage.

An exposed nerve howling in the cold.

The ravaged remains of a body torn apart and scattered to the four corners of the earth. There is no center. I cannot hold, cannot survive, cannot endure another moment of—

I gasp, emerging from the nightmare like breaking the surface of the water—one moment I'm drowning, the next all is as it should be.

I'm back. I'm myself, the old Eliza who couldn't smell danger or fear, who had one body, one skin, one reliable, human-sized heart she could count on not to fall in love too hard or too fast.

Two weeks ago, I would have given almost anything to be this Eliza again.

But now...as Jamal falls to the ground, clutching a nasty wound to his fire-hurling forehead, and Leo and Rourke sprint toward me, I can't stop crying.

"I'm sorry," I say, throat going tight as Rourke sets to work freeing me from the ropes.

"Don't you dare apologize." Leo gently pulls the IV needle from my vein, pressing the hem of his flannel shirt against the wound with fear in his eyes. "This isn't your fault, Eliza."

"We should have been watching you more closely, love," Rourke says, tearing at a knot with a force that rends the thick rope in two. "We won't make the same mistake again. I swear it on my life."

"And on mine." Leo presses a kiss to my forehead as he wipes the tears from my cheeks with his thumbs. "Don't cry. Everything's going to be all right. We're going to get you to a hospital. One of ours, where they know—"

"It's too late," I cut in, trembling so hard I send Pearl clattering to the floor as the ropes fall away. "He changed me back. Eugene. I'm just me again."

Leo blinks, but barely a second passes before he says, "But you're okay? You're not in pain anymore?"

I shake my head, sending more tears streaming onto my hot face. "No, but I'm human. Just a normal person. I c-can't break the curse."

"Fuck the fucking curse," Rourke says, his voice as rough as the arm he slips around my shoulders is tender. "Let the curse take our shivers and good fucking riddance to the both of them."

Leo wipes my cheeks with his sleeve, his eyes never leaving mine as he nods. "Agreed. I'm stepping down as second in line to the master throne tomorrow. And if Gloria tries to stop me, I'll give her the war she asked for tonight when she sent her man to kidnap you."

"Oh, Leo." Fresh pain floods into me as I remember the terrible truth. "She killed your wife. Gloria did. She told me so herself, right before she left. I'm so sorry."

Misery ripples across Leo's face, followed closely by rage and then a cold, razor-sharp determination that banishes my tears in a way his kindness and compassion could not.

This is what I needed to see, I realize—Leo strong and ready to take vengeance—to know that Gloria hasn't destroyed him.

"Then it's too late for stepping down," Rourke says, fire burning in his eyes. "We have to cut her out like the cancer she is. Now. Before she hurts anyone else. My master will help. As soon as Hamish learns what happened, we'll have all the resources of the Famine shiver at our disposal."

"But Hamish will still try to stop this." Leo helps me to my feet, bracing me against his side when my tingling legs threaten to give way. "He won't want us to choose Eliza. Not if she can't break the curse."

"We could go get Eugene." I motion toward the back of the large room, where I can now make out a pair of heavy double doors. "He just left, and he's not very fast. We can catch him, head to his lab, and make him change me back again."

Rourke shakes his head. "Not a chance, love. It's too risky."

"No, it's not, I made it through the change the first time, no problem. And he said there have been complications with his other subjects, but I wouldn't have to stay a rhino forever. I could just go shifter long enough to break the curse and then—"

"It's not an option, Eliza," Leo cuts in firmly. "The chances that you'd survive more DNA revisions without major damage and long-lasting consequences are slim to none."

"But I—"

He silences me with a finger pressed to my lips. "No. We won't risk you. You're too important."

"But I'm not," I say, my eyes stinging again. "Not anymore. I'm just an ordinary person."

"Not to me." Rourke moves closer, cupping my face in his hands. "To me, you're still the sun."

"And to me," Leo says. "I don't care what you are,

Eliza Frank. Rhino or woman or something in between, I would love you."

"You mean..." I swallow hard, too overcome to believe what I'm hearing. "You still want me? Just...me?"

"Just you," Leo confirms. "Wonderful, sweet, frustrating, adorable you."

"Ditto," Rourke says. "Except for the frustrating part. I don't find you frustrating, love. That's why I'm going to be your favorite husband. Wait and see. Maybe not today, or tomorrow, but eventually you're going to realize I'm the best."

"Keep telling yourself that, friend," Leo says. "It'll make the sting of solitude easier to bear when Eliza's sleeping in my bed to escape your snoring."

"I do not snore," Rourke protests.

"Beg to differ." Leo leans down, adding in a whisper for my ears only, "It's loud enough to wake the undead. If you ever want to sleep the night through again, you'll have to send him to his room before lights-out."

My lips tremble into a smile. "Or I could invest in some earplugs."

"All right, so I snore," Rourke says, his expression softening. "But this talk about earplugs is encouraging..."

"Be ours, Eliza," Leo says, brushing back the hair escaping from my bun as I tilt my head to look up into his dear face. "Let us love you. Give us a reason to fight for the future."

I nod, throat tight and eyes filling for what feels like the hundredth time. "Yes. I will, and I'll love you right back, with all of my heart."

"Then what do you say about taking our vows now, love? Preferably before Leo and I burst into flames?" Rourke peers warily at the horizon, now fully aglow and promising the arrival of the sun sooner than any of us would like.

"The car's outside, Rourke and I will be safe in the trunk," Leo assures me before my pulse can start racing again. "But Rourke's right. If we take the vows now, before we meet with his master tonight, it will be too late for anyone to try to talk us into putting shiver concerns first."

"Or to try to kill you to keep us from choosing love over curse-breaking," Rourke says with an apologetic shrug. "I'd like to say my master is above that sort of thing—I truly think he is—but probably best not to take any chances."

I nod. "All right. Let's do it." I step away from Leo, wiping my damp palms on my robe, hesitating as a thought zips through my mind. "But if I'm a vampire, too, who's going to drive the getaway car?"

"You won't be a vampire," Leo says. "We couldn't change you now, even if you wanted the Blood Kiss. We're still cursed and likely to remain that way for the near future."

I shake my head as I wince. "Right. Sorry. It's been a long night."

"It's fine, Princess Pea. And the vows *will* change you, binding your life force inextricably to ours," Rourke adds. "A three-way bond is special, different than the usual vows. As long as we're living, you'll remain alive, too, not appearing to age a day from the moment we form our bond."

"But if either of us were to die," Leo warns, "then you would die, too. So these promises aren't without risk, especially in a world as dangerous as ours."

"Nothing in life is without risk. But some are worth taking." I reach for Leo's hand and then Rourke's, the last of my doubt fading away as that where-I'm-meant-to-be sensation flows through me again.

These men are home to me, and I never want to leave it—or them—again.

"I'm ready," I say. "I want to be yours before the sun comes up."

Leo squeezes my hand. "You won't regret it. I'll make sure of it."

"We both will, but for the vows to be consecrated, we'll need a witness." Rourke's eyes narrow as he turns to where Jamal is lying curled in a ball on the floor, whimpering so softly I didn't hear him until now.

"He can be our witness." I roll my shoulders back. "And then we can tie him up in the back seat, and I'll drop him off at the nearest hospital. Let them figure out what to do with a third-eye wound."

"You're a kinder person than I am," Rourke says. "I'm in the 'leave him here to rot' camp, but…"

"He can't hurt anyone now." Leo crosses to stand above the clearly broken man. "He's lost his gift and his status in the shiver all in one day. But if I ever see you in Seattle again, Jamal…"

"I'll stay away," Jamal whispers from the floor. "But there's something you should know, majesty. Before you say your vows."

"Don't listen to him," Rourke growls. "He'll do anything to court favor and save his sorry skin."

"He's right." Jamal pushes into a seated position, tears in his human eyes and a pink trail running from beneath his curly bangs. "But I also tell the truth. And I think this is a truth you'll want to know before you take your mate." His attention shifts my way, a rueful smile lifting one side of his lips. "It was the last thing I saw. The last thing I'll ever see."

Rourke starts to speak, but I lift a hand, "No, let him tell us. It might be something we need to know."

Leo nods. "Quickly, then. We don't have much time before sunrise."

"We had it wrong, all of us, for all these years," Jamal says, with a soft laugh. "It was never about finding a one-in-a-million woman. It was about finding the woman who's one-in-a-million to our princes. *Your* Incomparable, the woman neither of you wants to live without."

Rourke and Leo exchange loaded glances before Rourke turns back to Jamal, voice hard as he demands, "You're serious? This isn't a trick?"

"I'm serious." Jamal arches a brow as he adds in a warning tone, "So be prepared. If you take your vows, you'll break a curse. By the time you wake this evening, all hell will have broken loose. You'll be the reigning masters and consort of Seattle, and the fate of our city will be in your hands."

Leo and Rourke lock eyes for another long beat before they turn to look at me, a single unspoken question scrawled across their handsome faces.

I curl my fingers into fists and smile. "Well, I have been wanting to do a little hiring and firing around the castle."

Leo grins as he reaches for me. "As soon as the dust clears, I'm putting you in charge of staffing."

"Even though I have no experience running an estate?" I move into his arms, hugging him tight.

"I trust your instincts," he says, claiming my lips for a long, slow kiss.

"As do I." Rourke shifts behind me, his arms going around my waist as he kisses my neck. "But as soon as the madness passes, the first item of business is the honeymoon. I need more time with nothing to do but feed and bed you, woman."

"Agreed," Leo says. "But we should hurry. As much as I hate to rush something like this, the sun is so close I can smell it."

"I'll start," Rourke says, fingers digging deeper into my waist. "With free will and by the power of the Kiss that grants eternal life, I, Reagan O'Rourke choose Eliza Frank as my consort and mate. I vow to defend our bond to the death, sharing her equally and honestly with Leo Poplov, my brother in this bond."

With a soft sigh of relief, Leo repeats the vow, sending shivers across my skin as he places his hands on my ribs just above Rourke's, making me ache for them. Even now, after this horrible night and with Jamal bleeding at our feet, I want them so badly it makes my voice shake as I stumble through my vow, repeating the words after Leo, promising to love and defend these men until the end of time.

The moment I've finished, a shimmering, sizzling sensation ripples through me, leaving me even more connected to Leo and Rourke, so close I can sense the echoes of their heartbeats pulsing beneath my skin.

For a commitment-phobe with serious intimacy issues, it should be a scary feeling. But I'm not scared. Even with all the danger looming in our near future, I'm excited, energized, and so grateful that when Leo and Rourke embrace, snuggling me between them as the bond settles into place, I almost start crying again.

But I don't. This time, happiness wins.

I hope it's the start of a trend.

"Are you sure I can't interest you in my services?" Jamal asks a few minutes later, on our way down to the car. "I may not have second sight anymore, but I know my way around the castle."

"Thanks, but no thanks," I say, watching as Leo and Rourke tie the shorter man in the same ropes he used to bind me and then tuck him into the back seat. "I appreciate you saving my life when the Kin Born attacked, but I'm going to stick with Sven. He might be honest to a fault, but at least he's honest."

Leo slams the door on Jamal before hurrying around to the back, where Rourke is holding open the trunk. "You're sure you know where to go? And what to do if any of Gloria's day guards find you before nightfall?" he asks, climbing inside.

"I've got it all under control," I say, shooing him on. "Now go. Rest. I'll see you at sunset."

"Hang in there, love," Rourke says, "and we'll get to the happily ever after part before you know it."

But it's all happily ever after, it turns out. Even the hard stuff.

After all, if I hadn't been going through hell, I never would have found heaven. I never would have been invited to stay at the castle or have escaped to a magical lighthouse where Leo, Rourke, and I had the time and space to finish falling in love.

So as I gun the 911 to life and peel out toward downtown, I'm not thinking of some far-off future when everything will be perfect *someday*.

I'm right here, in this sweet moment, with my new husbands safe in my trunk and a powerful machine humming around me, ready to take me exactly where we need to be.

CHAPTER 25

From the texts of
Eliza Frank Poplov-O'Rourke
and Eugene Eustace

Eliza: I don't care how dangerous it is, Eugene. I need you to find Leerie. ASAP. And just FYI, if you ignore my texts again, I will track you down and stab you with sharp pins until you remember that I'm married to two men who are just looking for an excuse to munch on your scrawny neck.

Eugene: I haven't forgotten, Eliza. Believe me. But it's not as easy as you're making it out to be. The Fairy research wing is guarded twenty-four seven, and even if I manage to slip past the guards, you need an approved thumbprint scan to access the database. My print won't give me clearance.

Eliza: Then find a friend or a thumb that will and get busy, buddy. You have forty-eight hours.

Eugene: That's impossible! There's no way I can get what you need by then.

Eliza: And there's no way I can wait any longer. Leerie's been missing for almost three weeks already. Her relatives have no idea where she is, and neither do any of her friends around here. She could be hurt, lost and alone somewhere, and sadly, you're our only hope of finding her. So step up and do the right thing for once in your miserable life, Eugene. You might find you enjoy it.

Eugene: I'll try. But if I get caught and the scary people running the fairy research program kill me, I'm coming back to haunt you, Eliza. And I don't plan on being a friendly ghost.

Eliza: Well, you haven't been a very friendly alive person, either, so that makes sense. Call you soon. Have good news for me, okay? If you do, I'm pretty sure I can make a case for calling off those guards outside your apartment and giving you some privacy again.

Eugene: Does that mean I can leave Seattle? Start fresh somewhere where the vampires don't know my name and want to kill me?

Eliza: Maybe. Give me Leerie's location, and then we'll talk about yours.

Eugene: Done. And Eliza?

Eliza: Yes?

Eugene: Good luck tonight. You deserve to win. You're the best of those pageant princesses. You always have been.

Eliza: Thanks, Eugene. Good luck to you, too. And just for the record, I forgive you for the rhinoceros thing. I can't say I enjoyed it all, but it's part of the journey that got me to where I am now, and I wouldn't trade that for anything.

Eugene: Even with the lingering side effects?

Eliza: Even with the lingering side effects. In fact, those may be my favorite part.

CHAPTER 26

ONE WEEK LATER

I'm not a cheater. I'm just not built that way.

It's not in my DNA—before or after the scrambling.

I've never slipped bleach into another pageant contestant's shampoo or stolen her fire batons before she's due on stage for the talent competition. I've never spiked a rival's health shake with ex-lax or put pepper spray in her makeup. I wouldn't so much as snip a line of beads from an evening gown, let alone use top-secret supernatural powers to give myself an unfair advantage.

Yes, a mini earthquake during Scrawny Sheila's dance routine—the only other ballet performance, and my only serious competition for first in the talent division—would have been convenient, but I'm an honorable woman. The day I discovered my lingering rhino gift, I vowed that I would only use my power for good, and it's a promise I intend to keep.

But as I stand beside the other winners on a raised platform in the lobby of the Seattle Suites hotel, holding my most dazzling smile for the flashing cameras, the temptation to put my foot down gets worse with every passing minute.

On one side of me, Sandra, second runner-up this year, keeps tripping over her feet as we change poses, jabbing her high heel into my instep more than once. On my other side, Penelope, the new Miss U.S., whispers nonstop smack between her Vaseline-coated teeth, testing the better angels of my nature.

"Must be so hard," Penelope coos in her syrupy sweet voice, "to know you lost because of something as stupid as a tragic haircut."

Ignoring her, I lift my chin and roll my left shoulder back, the better to display the first runner-up ribbon draped across my chest.

Do I wish I'd won? Yes. Does it stink that people still have such a narrow definition of what's beautiful in this day and age? Of course. But I overcame a lot of adversity to make it to this pageant, and I'm proud of myself, even if I'm not going home with prize money or a crown.

"I mean, what were you thinking?" Penny giggles—meanly. "What parasite took over your brain and made you think doing that to yourself was a good idea?"

"Your hairdresser should be shot," Sandra announces in a weary voice from my other side. "No offense. I mean, you still beat me, but..."

"None taken." I squeeze Sandra's hand. "Are you finally going off that horrible diet now? You seem so tired."

Sandra nods. "I am. I'm done with pageants and dieting and letting dress size and lack of butt-dimples mean more than anything else in my life. I'm checking into a treatment facility tonight."

"I'm so glad to hear it," I say, smile widening as we shift positions and lift our chins, obeying the photographers' shouted orders. "It'll be good to see you healthy."

"You should join her, Eliza," Penny says. "Clearly you need an intervention as much as Psycho Sandra."

"Shut it, Penelope," I snap, fighting to keep my smile pleasant. I search the crowd, looking for two familiar heads, but there's still no sign of Leo or Rourke. But the sun only set thirty minutes ago, and my husbands are coming from the Famine shiver's compound outside of town. We've been staying there since taking power, playing it safe until we're sure the Strife castle has been cleared of booby traps, traitors, and Gloria's ear collection.

I'm turning her tower trophy room into a breakfast nook, where non-vamp guests can watch the sunrise over the hills in the mornings, decorating it in peaceful, creepy-severed-ear-vibe-banishing blue and green.

"No, you shut it, Eliza," Penny says. "I'm on top now. You're just a washed up has-been who will never wear a crown."

I laugh at that, I can't help it.

"You think that's funny?" Penny glares at me beneath her gaudy rhinestone tiara.

"I do, actually." I have to wear a crown tonight, in fact, at the inauguration ceremony for the newly united Strife and Famine shivers. It's a Famine shiver heirloom from the sixteenth century, smuggled over in a cask of whiskey when they moved from Ireland to the Washington coast in the late eighteen hundreds.

It's a ceremonial piece—I won't have to wear three pounds of diamonds on my head all of the time, thank goodness. But for a night, paired with a shimmery silver dress that makes me look like I've been stitched up in moonlight...

Well, I'll take that crown.

And the two men in tuxes threading their way through the crowd toward me right now, looking so drop-dead gorgeous I always feel like the biggest winner in any room, no matter what my pageant banner reads.

Though, I'm pretty sure I'm done with banners and beauty pageants and all the bullshit that goes along with them. I'll just have to find another way to raise my start-up money.

Maybe there's a market for hundred-year-old vampire ears on eBay...

Or I could just take my husband's start-up check and thank him for believing in me—a much more reasonable option. Besides, it feels good to help and be helped by the people you love. I learned that the hard way, and it's a lesson I won't soon forget.

"Go ahead, yuck it up," Penny sneers, the smile falling from her face like a piano dropped out a third-story window now that the photographers are putting their cameras away. "But it's over for you, Eliza. You made a fool out of the entire pageant. You'll never qualify next year, even if you can grow out that mangy scraggle on your head by fall."

"Why are you being so mean?" Sandra sags onto a bench beside the Miss U.S. display at the back of the platform. "You won, Penny. Ease up."

"Ease up," Penny mimics in a high-pitched voice as

Leo and Rourke reach our side of the lobby, pausing at the base of our makeshift stage beside a cardboard cut-out of last year's Miss U.S. to watch the pageant fur fly. They've recently been through a nasty change of power —they know what one looks like.

"Seriously, Sandra," Penelope continues with a deceptively casual toss of her hair, a sure sign that a real zinger's on its way out of her wretched mouth. "If I were you, I'd skip that halfway house or whatever. Being thin is basically the only thing you have going for you. Lose that, and you're just another sad, ugly duckling, waddling around, thinking someday you're going to wake up and find out you're a swan."

"Enough, Penny," I growl, glaring a hole in her stupid, mean-spirited face.

"Spoiler alert," she crows, snapping her fingers in the air above poor Sandra's little head. "You're not." She shifts her glittering blue eyes my way. "And neither are you."

Parting shots delivered, Penny executes a runway-worthy one-eighty swivel with a hip pop and flounces away, headed off the platform and down to where the Miss U.S. handlers are waiting to whisk her away for a night of promotional interviews and photo ops—right after she cuts the first slice of the anniversary cake, celebrating one-hundred and fifty years of the Miss U.S. Pageant.

The cake is already waiting at the bottom of the stairs by Bonnie, the pageant organizer, and a man in a chef's hat holding a plate and a rhinestone-studded pastry server.

At the bottom of the stairs...

Right beneath Penny the Dreadful...

Heart racing and temptation rising to a feverish pitch inside of me, I glance at Sandra and the tears running down her pale face, then back at Penny, then back down to Sandra, her shoulders curving as she curls into herself like a frost-shriveled leaf.

And that does it.

I can't control it. My foot has a mind of its own.

I'm dimly aware of Leo calling my name in that warning tone of his, but it's too late, I've already summoned the power of the crash into my toes and brought down my Thunder Foot.

The platform ripples, shaking Sandra in her seat. She reaches out to brace herself on the arm of the bench, but unfortunately for Penny, there are no bench arms on the stairs. No railing, either.

So as the platform shakes, Penny trembles, losing her footing in her sky-high heels. She stumble-skids down the last few steps, gaining momentum until she's moving so fast there's no way she'll be able to stop herself before impact. She's going in, and she's going in hard.

I see the same realization zip across the chef's face a moment before he decides to jump for cover instead of going down with Penny in a blaze of buttercream frosting.

"Smart man," I murmur, hiding my grin behind my hand as Penelope collides with the cake, chest first, with a *glurp-pop* and a wail of misery as overly dramatic as it is satisfying. It's just cake, for goodness sake. It's not like I knocked her boobs-first into a vat of boiling oil.

"Oh my God," Sandra says, giggling beside me. "How did you do that?"

I blink innocently. "Me?"

Sandra's eyes narrow on my face. "Yes, you. You've been different this year, Eliza. The others may not have noticed, but I did. You're stronger. More grounded. And you're always smiling like you've got this amazing secret rolling around in your head, helping you stay above all the petty shit."

"Not above it, just...more resilient against it, I guess." I glance down at Rourke and Leo—who is trying to look disapproving about me using my powers in public after we discussed keeping a low profile, but who is also fighting a smile—and sigh. "Love is even more amazing than the stories, Sandra. I highly recommend it."

A wistful expression floats across her face. "Yeah? That's good to hear. I hope I find it someday. Though right now I would settle for a magic carpet to carry me down the stairs. I'm so crazy tired."

"Then lean on me, sister."

She lifts her hands and shakes her head, but I insist. "That's what we're here for, babe. To help each other and love each other and occasionally knock a bitch into a cake because she's in serious need of an attitude adjustment."

Giggling, Sandra says, "I knew it. You'll have to teach me your trick sometime. I want to be able to knock people into cakes."

"Maybe someday," I lie as I help her down the stairs and over to her mom and dad, who are waiting to take her somewhere to get the help she needs.

I can't give Sandra the power of my Thunder Foot, but I will absolutely be cheering her on every step of her recovery.

"First runner-up looks good on you," Rourke says, looping an arm around my waist as he, Leo, and I head for the exit, leaving Penelope behind us, still sputtering and weeping and scooping cake out of her cleavage. "You aren't too disappointed, then?"

I shake my head, taking Leo's hand. "Nah. I'm just glad it's over. I'm ready to spend some quality time with people I actually like. And to eat cake that hasn't had a jerk's face in it."

Rourke stifles a laugh. "Oh dear Lord, that was priceless. That wee wretch deserved it, though. That and more."

"And she didn't look nearly as lovely in a crown as you do." Leo squeezes my fingers as we step out into a perfect early summer night, bound for the limo idling at the curb. "Are you ready to be crowned as the first human shiver queen?"

"Yes." I sigh happily. "And to dance all night."

"Not all night, I hope," Rourke says, with a sniff. "I've reserved the penthouse at the hotel, and the Pierre prides itself on its obscenely large beds."

"Obscene, eh?" I smile as Leo opens the limo door.

"Truly appalling," Rourke assures me, his eyes dancing. "You'd have room for three or four husbands in one of those. If you were of the mind to collect that many."

"I find the two I've got are just fine, thank you," I say, sliding into the back seat with a furrowed brow. "Though, it's been so long since I had them both at the same time, I could be wrong. Maybe I could handle three…"

"Over my sun-ravaged corpse," Leo mutters, gliding in beside me and pulling me into his arms for a deep, hard, absolutely thrilling kiss.

"Move over, you selfish things." Rourke tumbles in between us, and I giggle as he pulls me into his lap with an enthusiasm that sends us both tumbling to the floor.

I half expect Leo to order us both to behave, but instead, he slams the door, orders the driver to hit it, and rolls onto the spacious floor beside us. He works open the buttons at the side of my gown and Rourke cups my breasts as the fabric falls free. And then Leo's lips are claiming mine, and my dress has magically vanished, and Rourke's cock presses between the cheeks of my ass.

Soon, I lose track of who is touching me where, giving myself over to the hot rush of love and lips and teeth and tongue and hands giving and taking pleasure so sweet that by the time I take Leo into my mouth as Rourke pushes into me from behind, I'm lost to pleasure.

Drunk and divine and soaring so high I never want to come down.

But I do. At least for a little while.

Long enough to get dressed in our fancy penthouse suite and attend the ball, escorted by the two most handsome men in the world. We make our promises to our people, renew our vows to each other, and welcome four new baby vamps into our shiver with Strife and Famine hoodie sweatshirts—my idea, and much cozier swag than the drop of blood in a tiny vase that Leo insists we give away as well, as a nod to tradition.

I'm happy for the new vampires, but happy to remain human myself. For now, at least. I like knowing I can be awake when my men can't, that I can protect them and watch over them and be their eyes and ears until the sun goes down.

And I really do look so much better with a little bit of a tan, a fact Leo confirms as he traces my bikini lines in our suite later, insisting they make me, "even more beautiful."

"Naked, but better," Rourke agrees, pressing a kiss to my hip that makes my blood rush.

"And I'd like you both better naked, too," I say, leading the way to the bedroom with my heart full of love. "Right now."

I'm still worried about Leerie and the unstable state of our newly combined shivers and global chaos and war and poverty and all the suffering I can't do a damned thing to fix. But I'm also committed to living every moment of my life to the fullest, hanging on to every beam of light, and holding strong in the darkness.

And orgasms.

I'm committed to having as many of those as possible.

"Five," I whisper to Leo as he pushes me back onto the bed. "I want five."

And he and Rourke deliver like *whoa*, proving that what you actually get can sometimes be even more amazing than what you thought you wanted. Also, that it's totally true—once you go vamp, you don't go back.

At least I won't, not today or tomorrow or any day in the long and lovely future I'll share with the men I love.

Sign up for Bella's newsletter and never
miss a sale or new release. Subscribe Here.

Keep reading for a sneak peek of
UNLEASHED
a red hot reverse harem romance
out now!

ABOUT THE BOOK

One woman on the run. Four dangerously sexy bodyguards. And a war brewing that will change the shifter world forever...

I'm living on borrowed time, fighting for survival against a deadly new virus that has no cure and a cult doing its best to brainwash me. But when a mysterious note shows up on my windowsill one night, its chilling message--*Run, Wren*--launches me out of the frying pan and into the fire.

Within hours, everything I thought I knew about my life, my family, and my origins is obliterated, and I'm racking up enemies at an alarming rate. Between the cult I've just escaped, a violent shifter faction out for my blood, and an ancient evil who eats "chosen ones" like me for breakfast, my last hope is to join forces with four dangerous-looking men who claim they were sent to guard my life.

Luke, a werewolf with a rap sheet. Creedence, a lynx shifter who never met a mark he couldn't con. Kite, a bear kin with a mean right hook and heart of gold. And Dust, my childhood best friend and dude voted least likely to be a secret shape-shifting griffin.

But are these men really what they seem?

Or are my alpha guardians hiding a secret agenda of their own?

I'm not sure, but one thing is for certain—choosing the right allies will mean the difference between life and death. For me, and everyone I love.

UNLEASHED is book one in the Dark Moon Shifter's series. It is a true reverse harem featuring one woman and her four mates.

CHAPTER ONE
Wren

I don't believe in ghosts. I don't believe in ghosts. I don't—
Believe.
In ghosts.
Palms sweating and a sour taste rising in my throat, I stand tall, forcing a smile to my face for the next girl in the cafeteria serving line.

She has red hair and moon-glow skin just like Scarlett. But she isn't Scarlett.

She isn't, she isn't, she isn't...

This is just my virus-addled brain playing tricks on me.

I refuse to get my hopes up. I know better. After eight years and a dozen cases of mistaken identity—racing after a woman boarding a train or taking a stranger's hand at the farmer's market—I know my sister is never coming back to me.

Scarlett is gone. Forever.

Scarlett is dead, and I don't believe in ghosts. Only the kooky extremists and the old hippies in our church actually believe in things that go bump in the night and exorcisms and all the rest of the crazy. The rest of the Church of Humanity movement is firmly grounded in reality and helping people come together to make a better world.

Which means not scaring away newbies to the movement by rushing up to hug them like they're your long-lost best friend.

As the girl slides her tray closer, her blurred features come into sharper focus, revealing a forehead that's too wide, a nose that's too sharp, and blue eyes instead of brilliant, glittering green. She isn't Scarlett, but the sadness dragging at her delicate features reminds me of my sister, and my throat goes tight as I ask her, "Beef stew or veggie?"

"Um...either one is fine, thanks," she whispers, ducking her head to hide behind a shock of dirty auburn hair. "Whatever."

"Well, I can't get enough of the veggie. The tofu has

great flavor," I say gently, "but I'd love for *you* to choose. I want to make sure you get what you'd like best. Your opinion matters."

The girl looks up sharply, suspicion blooming in her tired eyes. I smile in response, silently assuring her this isn't a prank and I'm not being a smartass B-word. I truly care about her opinion and her preferences. I care about *her* and every teen who comes into the Rainier Beach C of H shelter.

After three years as an assistant coordinator, this is *my* shelter now. And in my shelter, every soul is precious and valued. Any staff members who thought differently were relocated when I took the reins last August. And I intend to hold on tight to those reins through this relapse and all the pain, dizziness, and exhaustion that goes with it.

I may only be able to work part-time, but the hours that I am here, I'm all in.

When Lance, one of our regulars, sighs heavily behind the new girl and grumbles, "Just pick something already," I shoot him a gentle, but firm, look and say, "It's fine, Lance. We're not in any rush." I glance back at the girl. "What's your name, honey?" I just got here an hour ago and haven't had time to look over the new intake forms.

"Ariel," she mumbles, glancing nervously between Lance and me.

"Like the mermaid." I grin. "That was my favorite cartoon when I was little. My sister has pretty red hair like yours, and she would let me brush it while we watched and sang along with all the songs."

Ariel's lips curve shyly. "That's my sister's favorite

princess, too." She blinks, her smile vanishing as quickly as it appeared. "Or, at least it was. I haven't seen her in a couple of years. Not since my stepdad kicked me out."

I want to hurry around the counter, pull her into my arms, and promise her things are going to be better for her from now on. She's at a Church of Humanity Shelter, not one of the poorly funded nightmares on the east side of town. No one will hurt her here. No one will judge her. It's finally safe for her to grieve and grow and begin to heal from all the horrible things she's no doubt been through as a beautiful young girl living on the streets of post-Meltdown Seattle.

But I've learned to keep my heart off my sleeve and my touchy-feely hugging instincts in check.

A lot of the kids in my care have yet to learn the difference between touch that offers comfort and touch that makes demands—sometimes ugly demands. Until they make it clear a hug is welcome, I keep my hands to myself.

Instead I lean in and whisper confidentially, "I bet Ariel is still her favorite. Once you go mermaid, you never go back. I still have mermaid pictures on my wall and I'm a grown woman." I cast a glance at Lance as I add with mock seriousness. "But keep that just between us, okay? Gotta keep my street cred."

"What street cred?" Lance snorts. "It's too late, Miss Frame. We all know you're a hopeless cheese case by now. The secret's out. Now give the girl some stew before she passes out." He nudges Ariel's arm gently with his elbow. "You're starving, right?"

Ariel laughs softly and nods. "Yeah. I am." She grins

across the counter at me, hope cautiously creeping into her eyes. "I'll have the beef stew, please. I'm a meat eater in a big way."

"A girl after my own heart," Lance booms, making Ariel laugh again as she scoots her tray down toward the dessert station. "Two servings of beef for me, please, Miss F. I'm starving after all that nature exploration shit today."

"Language," I admonish, but my heart isn't in it. Lance came to us an angry street kid with two misdemeanors for drug possession and a history of taking out his frustration with life on smaller teens. After six months, he's become a kind young man who enjoys helping the newbies at the shelter fit into our rhythms and who volunteers for campus clean up and laundry duty without being asked.

All it took to unlock his heart was for someone to show him how to turn the key. He just needed someone to care about him first, to show him he was worth it, so he could start learning how to love himself and others. It's simultaneously so simple and so hard, and I'm so, so proud of him.

"You're doing great, Lance." I mound his tray with as much stew as I can fit into the main compartment on his plate. "I appreciate the light you shine around here."

Lance's cheeks go pink beneath his golden-brown skin as he rolls his eyes. "Yeah, yeah, Miss F, don't get sappy on me. Trying to play it cool in front of the new girls."

"You know the policy on inter-shelter dating, Lance," I remind him, arching a brow.

"Yeah, yeah." He flashes a bright-white smile over

his shoulder as he slides his tray away. "But a guy can dream. I won't be here forever, you know."

The words make my chest ache. It's true. He won't be here forever. That's the hardest part of my job—falling in love with these kids and then seeing them go off to foster families, most often never to return.

I don't blame them for wanting to leave the past in the past and move on with their lives, but that doesn't keep me from missing them. From wondering where they are and wishing we could stay one big extended family.

But that's part of my own set of mental glitches—I hate for people to leave. Too many people have left me already. First the biological mother and father I can't remember, then my best friend, Dust, and finally my sister, the person who meant the most to me in the world. She was my hero, my protector, my playmate, and my confidante. She was everything I wanted to grow up to be, even though she never made it past the age of nineteen.

I've been thinking of her more than ever recently.

For a time, years after the fire, I was able to put her out of my mind for days, sometimes even weeks, and go about my life.

But now...

Now my health is failing the same ways hers failed.

Now there are days when I can't get out of bed, the agony burning through my bones is so bad.

There are moments—flashes of despair—in which I consider taking a few too many steps at the edge of the train platform. I don't want to die, but I don't know how much longer I can live with the pain, the weakness, the uncertainty of whether I will ever go back into remission.

The virus my drug-addict bio-mom caught from a dirty needle and passed on to both of her daughters is a Meltdown disease, one of the many exotic new autoimmune viruses that oozed out of the polar ice caps as they melted to near nothingness in the years before I was born. Researchers and scientists are working as fast as they can to find cures for the Devour virus and the other diseases plaguing humanity, but a cure is still decades away.

I won't live to see it. Not unless there's a miracle.

There are days when that's okay with me, when I'm grateful that there will soon be a day when I won't have to drag my body out of bed, stuff my mouth full of ten different kinds of meds, and fight to pass as a normal, functional adult anymore.

And then there are days like today, when I look out at a cafeteria filled with once hopeless kids, now laughing and chatting and eating with the gusto of healthy people who need fuel for all the big things they're going to do with their lives, and I pray for another year.

Two.

Three or more—if somehow my body can be convinced to stop attacking itself.

"We good to close the line, boss?" a voice rumbles softly from beside me, making my cheeks heat.

That's what he does to me, this man who is another reason I would like to stick around a little longer. Long enough to see what having a steady boyfriend might be like, maybe...

Or at least long enough to see if Kite's kisses are as lovely as the hugs he gives me every evening as we say goodbye and head for our separate train stops.

"Yeah, let's close up." I turn, smiling up at him as whips off his hairnet with a relieved sigh, setting his long, glossy black hair free to stream around his broad shoulders. "Aw, poor Kite," I tease. "I'm telling you, you're pulling off the hairnet. It's a solid look for you. You should take a selfie."

His rich brown eyes narrow on mine. "Very funny, Bird Girl," he says, the nickname making me grin even wider. "Are we saving the peach cobbler, or can I pack up what's left for the staff?"

I glance over at the warming pan to see only a few inches of untouched cobbler. "Go ahead and wrap it up for the staff. You're going to make Carrie Ann's day. She lives for an excuse to have dessert for breakfast."

"Amen!" Carrie Ann, my right-hand woman, cruises by with an arm full of dirty salad bar dishes bound for the kitchen. Her blond bob is still safely secured under her hairnet and her face is makeup free, but she looks as adorable, a real-life pixie with a mischievous grin that always lifts my spirits. She flashes it now as she says, "Make mine a big one, Kite. My legs are jelly from that hike around the bay. I need sugar to restore me. Lots of it."

I keep my grin in place, refusing to feel envious of my friend or the others who were able to make the hike around the new beach line today, exploring the places where the rising ocean has intruded and where Seattle's manmade barriers to the overflow are holding strong.

Yes, I would have loved to spend hours out in nature

with Kite, absorbing his teachings on native flora and fauna, interspersed with the always fascinating stories passed down from his grandfather—former chief of the Samish Indian Nation—but I learned a long time ago not to waste energy feeling sorry for myself.

Besides, Kite will fill me in on our way to the train. He always does. My newest hire is not only a gentle giant with a heart of gold and a knack for winning over even the surliest street kid, he's also patient, generous, and thoughtful.

And gorgeous, a wayward voice whispers in my head.

I avert my gaze, pretending great interest in the chafing dishes as Carrie swoops in to grab the empty green bean container near my elbow. I'm not ready to let Kite see how much appreciation I have for his sculpted features, silky hair, and big, burly, and completely snuggle-perfect body. I have as many fantasies about curling up in Kite's arms and going to sleep with my head on his chest as I do about other, racier things. Maybe it's a side effect of being so tired all the time—nap fantasies are totally a thing for sicklies like me—but I don't think so.

I think it's a side effect of him being absolutely adorable.

"You need vegetables," Kite calls after Carrie as she scoffs and continues about her business. "For a grown woman, you're eating habits are shameful."

"Good thing I'm not done growing yet," Carrie Ann shoots back as the kitchen door swings closed behind her.

Kite turns to me with a sigh. "Someone needs to teach that girl the basics of good nutrition."

"I've tried," I say, turning off the warmers beneath the stew. "But she's set in her ways. Sugar, caffeine, and sliced deli meat are her three basic food groups. Maybe she'll rethink things when she's older. She's only twenty; she has time." I reach for the edges of the chafing dish, engaging my abs as I prepare to lift the metal container. It's half empty and can't weigh more than ten pounds, but I still struggle to work it free, sweat breaking out in the valley of my spine as I slide it to the edge of the counter.

"Here, let me." Before I can protest, Kite claims the meat dish in one hand and lifts the leftover tofu stew free with the other, making it all look as effortless as plucking a couple of summer cherries out of a bowl.

"I could have done it," I say, but Kite is already headed toward the kitchen.

"Just wipe down the serving line, boss," he calls back. "Let your minions take care of the heavy lifting."

He's clearly trying to dismiss my struggle with a joke, but it isn't funny. It's demoralizing, and the way my arms are trembling as I finish cleaning the serving line is enough to make me want to grind my teeth in frustration.

By the time Carrie Ann sidles up beside me, clutching her Tupperware container of cobbler, I'm fighting tears.

Like the sweetheart she is, she puts a hand on my back and reminds me, "You don't have to do any of this, you know. Kite, the others, and I are happy to do the grunt work."

I shake my head. "But I hate that. I feel like such a diva."

"Oh, please." Carrie laughs her bright, musical laugh, making a few of the kids seated nearby glance our way with smiles instinctively curving their lips.

That's what Carrie's laugh does to people, and one of the many reasons she's the best choice for my replacement when the time comes. Other people have more education and fancier degrees, but Carrie is an upbeat force of nature who lifts the spirits of everyone she meets.

And she knows exactly where these kids are coming from. Just four years ago, Carrie was one of them, one of the shattered souls that ended up on our doorstep after the rough streets of Seattle chewed her up and spit her out. But, lucky me, this time one of the new friends I'd made stuck around to join our crew on a more permanent basis.

"You're the farthest thing in the world from a diva," Carrie continues, gazing up at me. "You're the hardest working woman I know. And we need your brain and your heart more than we need your muscles. Seriously, when you come in tomorrow, sit your ass down in your office and give your energy to your counseling sessions. That's where you work the magic. Anyone can man the serving line, Wren—even Kite, though he clearly was never taught how to properly clean up after himself."

"I heard that," Kite calls from the bowels of the kitchen. "It's not my fault I have six older sisters who never let me in the kitchen."

Carrie rolls her eyes as she leans in to whisper, "Six older sisters. Can you imagine? I bet they used him as a dress-up doll when he was little."

"I heard that, too," Kite says, proving his hearing

really is something extraordinary. "And no, they didn't, but I did have to wear their clothes until I was too big to fit into them." He emerges from the kitchen, two containers of cobbler held lightly in one hand. "My mother couldn't see the point in wasting good money on boy clothes since I was the last baby on the docket."

Carrie giggles, and I smile as I say, "Aw. I would pay good money to see those baby pictures. You in ruffles."

"Stay on my good side, and I'll show them to you for free someday," he says with a wink that sends warmth flooding through my chest. He turns to Carrie with a mock glare and adds, "But not you, Trouble. I'd never hear the end of it from you."

"Correct," Carrie cheerfully agrees, pressing up onto tiptoe to peck my cheek. "See you tomorrow, Sunshine. Text me if you want to chat later. I'm just hanging at home tonight, hiding from my miserable roommates and the cockroaches. No money to go catch a band until next payday."

"Will do. Get home safe," I say, sweet anticipation dumping into my bloodstream as she departs, leaving me alone with Kite.

It's my favorite time of the day, the fifteen minutes it takes to walk to the place where our paths diverge on the way to our separate train stations. I look forward to it from the moment my eyes creak open in the morning.

There are days, when I wake up aching and feverish in a nest of sweaty covers and roll over to be sick in the bucket by my nightstand, when this walk is the only thing that gets me out of bed. This walk is the lifeline I cling to as I force my throbbing joints into the shower to sit on the stool Mom bought for me a few months ago when she realized I no longer had the strength to stand under the stream until my meds had kicked in.

Unless something changes, there will come a day—a day not far from this one—when I will no longer have the strength to make this walk, either. But it isn't today. Today I am still alive and upright, and my meds are holding the pain at bay enough for me to enjoy the way my blood pumps faster as Kite rests a warm hand on my shoulder and asks, "You ready, boss lady?"

I nod, beaming up at him. "I am. Just let me grab my jacket and I'll meet you out front."

I make my way slowly to my office, conserving my energy, wanting to save it all for the walk through the misty spring afternoon with Kite.

I may not have many afternoons like these left, but that isn't a reason for sadness. It's a reason to savor, to treasure, to soak up every minute of sweetness and pack it away for a day when I'll need good memories more than ever.

Unleashed is out now!

ABOUT THE AUTHOR

Bella Jacobs loves pulse-pounding action, fantasy, and supernaturally high stakes, mixed with swoon-worthy romance and unforgettable heroes. She's been a full time writer for over a decade and is deeply grateful for the chance to play pretend for a living.

She writes as Bella for her trips to the dark side and can't wait to take you on her next adventure.

Visit her at www.bellajacobsbooks.com

ALSO BY BELLA JACOBS

The Dark Moon Shifter Series

Unleashed

Untamed

Unbroken (Spring 2019)

Supernatural in Seattle Series

Fangs for Sharing

Hot as Howl (Leerie's Story-Summer 2019)

Made in the USA
Coppell, TX
26 January 2020